an impossible thing

A PRIDE AND PREJUDICE VARIATION

A GENTLEMAN'S FOLLY
BOOK 2

SOPHIA MURRAY

elizabeth bennet

IT HAD BEEN three months since that fateful day when Mr. Collins had proposed marriage to me.

I'd had no choice but to decline his offer—how could I have married him? But as my dear Mama kept reminding me, it was now my fault that Mr. Collins had turned on his heel and marched away from Longbourn to be welcomed with open arms to Lucas Lodge.

Now my dear friend Charlotte Lucas was Mrs. Collins and would be Mistress of Longbourn when my father died.

My mother was determined that I should never forget how my own selfishness had doomed our family.

But I refused to believe it.

At least… I tried to.

Coming to London was supposed to help ease the ache in my heart, and I was grateful to my aunt and uncle for welcoming me into their home. It was a quiet afternoon and the silence of the house, punctuated only by the muted noise from Gracechurch Street, was a much needed balm. The furnishings of the drawing room were comfortable yet modest, reflecting the sensible nature of my relations, and they were a far cry from the overstuffed and faded decor my mother had chosen to fill the rooms with at Longbourn.

I sat with a book in my lap, but my thoughts were far from its pages. Instead, they roamed the events of recent months, and I struggled to make sense of the tumultuous emotions that churned within me. I felt the weight of my family's expectations bearing down upon me, as much as I tried to defy them, yet I could not quiet the voice in my head that whispered of love and happiness, like a fairy tale not meant for the likes of me.

"Elizabeth, my dear," my aunt said, her soft voice interrupting my thoughts, "you seem rather preoccupied today. Is something troubling you?"

I sighed as I set aside my untouched book and looked into her kind eyes. "I must be honest with you," I said. "I cannot help but feel conflicted these days. With Mr. Collins married to Charlotte, I find myself questioning if there will ever be a gentleman who is truly worthy of my affection."

"Do you believe that you have made a mistake in refusing him?" she asked gently.

I made a face, which caused her to smile.

"No, indeed," I replied. "It is only— I do not know how to put it into words."

"Ah, my sweet niece," she said, taking my hand in hers and squeezing it gently. "I know you will not say it, but it must weigh upon you that Mr. Collins was able to pivot to Miss Lucas so..."

"Immediately?" I said wryly.

"Indeed," my aunt said. "But do not let the haste of Mr. Collins' actions cloud your vision. Your heart will know when you have found the right gentleman, one who shares your values and interests. A true partner."

"Thank you," I said, feeling a small measure of comfort from her words. Yet the tumult within me remained, as I considered

2

that I may have to marry a gentleman I did not love for the sake of my family's future.

"Lizzy," my aunt continued, "I know you may feel uncertain about your future, but remember that you are still young and have much time ahead of you. Trust in yourself and your judgment."

I attempted a smile. "I shall try to keep your wise words in mind."

"I know you are determined to marry for love, but I hesitate to mention that you may need to contemplate other factors..."

My aunt's words chilled me to the bone, and I stared into the dancing flames as if seeking their guidance. "I understand as well as anyone the importance of securing my family's future," I admitted, biting my lip. "But can one truly be content in a marriage without love?"

"Sometimes, sacrifices must be made for the greater good," she replied gently. "It is not an ideal situation, but we live in a world where practical concerns cannot be ignored. Miss Lucas made a practical decision, did she not?"

I nodded. "She did," I murmured.

My aunt's words weighed heavily upon my heart, and I felt the walls of my once hopeful dreams crumble around me. "Do you think it possible to find happiness in such a union?" I asked, desperate for reassurance.

"Perhaps not the same degree of happiness as in a love match," she conceded, "but there is something to be said for companionship and shared responsibilities. Over time, respect and affection may grow."

"Affection is not love," I whispered, my voice barely audible above the rhythmic ticking of the clock.

"True, but love is not the only ingredient for a successful marriage," my aunt reminded me. "Many couples learn to appreciate one another's qualities and build a life together despite the absence of passionate love."

"Is that what I must settle for, then?" I asked bitterly, struggling to accept the harsh reality before me. "A life devoid of the love I have always yearned for?"

"Lizzy, my dear girl, your future is your own to shape," she replied softly. "All I ask is that you consider every possibility and make the best decision for yourself... but do not forget your family."

I sighed, my heart heavy with the burden of my uncertain fate. "I could not forget if I tried," I said. The thought of marrying without love filled me with dread.

"Good," she said, squeezing my hand gently. "I know this is not an easy subject, but it is important to confront the realities of our world. Whatever you decide, always remember that you are loved and supported by those who care for you."

As our conversation faded into silence, the ticking of the clock on the mantelpiece seemed to grow louder, serving as a solemn reminder that time was slipping away, and with it, my chances of a happy future..

Despite my aunt's counsel, my heart remained heavy, and I could not shake the sense of unease that had settled upon me. Would I find love or be forced to make a difficult choice? Only time would tell. Perhaps, just perhaps, I would find that elusive gentleman who would cherish my heart as much as I cherished his.

My mind wandered back to the disastrous proposal from Mr. Collins, and how his pompous manner and misplaced attentions had repelled me. I could not bear the thought of becoming his wife, existing merely as a token of his social standing, and so I had sent him away.

Yet now, as I contemplated the alternative—a life of solitude or a burden on my poor family—I felt a pang of regret.

"Still," I continued, "I am confronted with the truth that the only other option available to me in Meryton seems to be the wife of a militia officer. A prospect which holds little appeal for me, either."

"Perhaps, my dear, the solution lies not in Meryton itself, but in expanding your horizons," my aunt suggested gently. "Perhaps you would wish to come to one of the season's balls? I am very certain that I could obtain an invitation if you would like to attend?"

My eyes widened. "Do you mean it?"

"Yes, of course," my aunt replied, her blue eyes sparkling with excitement. "It would be an excellent opportunity for you to meet some of the eligible gentlemen of London society."

My heart leaped with joy at the prospect of a new beginning, and for the first time in days, I felt a glimmer of hope. Perhaps my chance at love and happiness was not lost after all.

"As much as it would mean to me to have such an opportunity," I said, beaming with excitement, "I cannot help but feel that such an invitation would be difficult to come by."

"Nonsense," my aunt exclaimed. "Lady Bearing is a very close friend, and I have a feeling that she will agree that this is a necessary favor. I will have no trouble securing an invitation for you."

All at once, my enthusiasm faded and my aunt immediately sensed a change in my mood.

"What is it, my dear?"

"I— I have nothing suitable for a society ball," I said. "It is a kind thought, aunt. But I did not bring anything so fine as would be acceptable to Lady Bearing."

"Indeed, I shall find a solution," my aunt said with a wink. "Lady Bearing has a daughter of about your own age, or perhaps Jane's age, but I do not see why we might not be able to find a gown that would be more than suitable."

I felt a wave of relief wash over me at my aunt's offer. Perhaps attending a society ball could be the answer to my dilemma.

Excitement coursed through my veins, and I could hardly wait to see what lay ahead. "Thank you," I said, feeling grateful for her unwavering support.

She squeezed my hand once more, before rising from her chair and making her way towards the door.

"Then it is settled," she said. "In the morning we shall call upon Lady Bearing and set about mending this broken heart of yours."

I nodded, still musing over the possibility of finding love in London.

Perhaps my dream was not impossible, after all. I couldn't help but feel a renewed sense of hope and excitement for what the future held.

Perhaps it was foolish, or, perhaps it was fate that lay ahead of me.

* * *

AS MY AUNT HAD PROMISED, Lady Bearing was very welcoming and generous with the lending of a beautiful gown in a striking sapphire blue silk for the festivities ahead.

I was overwhelmed by Lady Bearing's gift and attention, but she insisted and I could not refuse her.

"My daughter will not be in attendance, unfortunately," Lady Bearing said with an air of irritation. "She is refusing to leave Bath for the season even though she knows that she will never find a suitable husband so far from London."

"My niece is hoping to make a match," my aunt mentioned casually. "Perhaps you might be so kind as to watch out for any gentlemen who might be of an... interesting temperament?"

Lady Bearing smiled and sipped her tea. The other woman was tall and statuesque, and would have been difficult to ignore even in a crowded ballroom. I had no doubt that her daughter was a beauty as well and I wished that she had been present in London so that I could meet her and thank her in person for the lending of her gown.

"Interesting temperament, you say..." Lady Bearing's eyebrow rose slightly. "And what sort of gentleman might you have in mind, Miss Bennet?"

"I— I do not know off hand," I stammered.

"A country gentleman, I should think," Mrs. Gardiner said with a smile. "Someone with an estate, and a goodly education, and a serious mind. A gentleman who rides but does not hunt, and someone who enjoys the quieter life that a country estate affords..."

"I see," Lady Bearing said. She looked at me carefully and a smile curved across her full lips. "I believe I might have someone in mind."

My heart beat strangely in my chest as my aunt nodded reassuringly. I was not certain that I wished to enter into any matchmaking schemes. I had had quite enough of my own mother's busy attention on that subject. But my aunt only had my best interests at heart, and perhaps I would be able to enjoy myself enough to distract from the heavy thoughts that had plagued my mind.

"AS I PREDICTED, you will be a striking sight," my aunt said as I came down the stairs. "The orange ribbon is a bold choice."

"I did not bring anything blue," I said. I had been self-conscious about the choice of the orange ribbon, but it looked well against my dark curls, and I could not deny that I wished to stand out at the ball. I could never do such a thing in Meryton, and it would have been shocking indeed to wear such a dark colored gown. It would look almost black in the candlelight so I would have to be careful about my choice of position in the ballroom.

Or perhaps I would throw caution to the wind. No one knew me in London, I could be anonymous and would be free to dance with anyone I pleased. They did not need to know that I had four sisters at home, each of them dependent in some way upon my choice of a husband.

They did not need to know that my Mama was high spirited and noisy in her opinions.

They did not need to know anything unless I deemed it necessary.

Tonight I could be unapologetically myself.

"You look beautiful," my aunt said with a smile. "Come, Lady Bearing will be overjoyed to see how well you look in her daughter's gown. I daresay Miss Bearing could not wear it so well as you."

My cheeks were already warm at my aunt's praise and I was suddenly pleased that Miss Bearing would not be at the ball. I could not bear it when my own mother praised one of my sisters or another young lady at the expense of another, and I had a feeling that Lady Bearing was adept at this practice as well.

The carriage ride to Bearing House was not a long one, but I used the journey to try and calm my nervous heartbeat and reassure myself that all would be well.

It was just one evening.

Just one.

Dancing. Rum punch. Opulent food. Candlelight.

And then it would be over and I would not have to think of it again.

two

LADY BEARING'S house had been a sight to behold in the daylight, but it had been transformed for the ball and its opulence and splendor beyond anything I had ever seen before. The entry foyer was adorned with lush velvet draperies and the ballroom had been similarly swagged and hung with heavy fabrics that set off the shimmering crystal chandeliers hung from the high ceiling.

More musicians than I had ever seen in Meryton were arranged in the corner of the ballroom, and they played a lively tune as couples swirled gracefully across the polished dance floor, laughter and chatter filling the air like sweet perfume.

My heart raced with anticipation as I entered the room, my silk gown rustling softly about my ankles. My hands felt clammy inside the gloves I had borrowed from Lady Bearing's daughter, but I refused to let my nerves get the better of me. This was my chance to prove that I could thrive in such distinguished company, and perhaps even secure a future for myself beyond the confines of Longbourn.

I glanced down at my gown, satisfied with my choice that Lady Bearing had made on my behalf. The deep blue was unique among the other ladies, and while it was not as ostentatious as some of the gowns I saw, it suited me well—simple and elegant, yet bold enough to make a statement.

As I stood, surveying the room, I couldn't help but feel a mix of excitement and apprehension. I was here for more than just the pleasure of dancing; this was an opportunity to forge connections and broaden my horizons, away from the constraints of my family and the expectations of society. It was my desire for independence and autonomy that drove me, even though the thought of navigating these shark-infested waters alone was daunting.

"Miss Bennet, there you are!" A young woman in a pale pink gown and a large brightly dyed ostrich feather in her hair rushed over to me. She was followed by four other young ladies, all dressed very finely in a gown of rich silk. They all wore welcoming smiles upon their faces, though I did not know any of them, they seemed to know me.

"I—"

"Lady Bearing has prevailed upon us to be your companions for the evening," the young lady in pink said brightly. "I am Miss Kelly, and these are Miss Grange, Miss Yarrow, Miss Peters, and Miss Brown."

I nodded to each of the ladies in turn, knowing that I would not be able to recall any of them if I were tested.

"Have you danced yet?" Miss Kelly asked.

"No—I have not," I said.

"It is for the best," Miss Kelly said with a grimace. "There is a desperate lack of decent gentlemen here this evening."

"And even fewer who are unmarried," Miss Grange said with a sigh. "But that does not bother you, does it Delilah?"

The one I guessed was Miss Peters frowned at her friend and pushed at her gently as the others laughed.

As the other young ladies chatted and gossiped I tried to

relax into their company. I was far too accustomed to the quiet company of Jane and Charlotte.

"Come, Miss Bennet, we must get some punch," Miss Kelly said suddenly. I nodded and allowed her to pull me along, but as we walked, I looked around the room and my gaze fell upon a tall gentleman with dark hair that curled over the collar of his fine shirt and dark eyes that seemed to look into my very soul. He was handsome, there was no doubt in my mind about that.

I paused briefly as he noticed me, and then Miss Kelly pulled on my arm and I resumed my progress across the ballroom toward the banquet tables.

"Oh, I am ever so excited," Miss Grange said as she rushed ahead and poured glasses of rum punch for all of us. "Lady Bearing's beverages are almost famous," she said with a smile. Miss Kelley handed me a glass and I stepped away from the other young ladies to watch the dance floor.

The punch was, indeed, delicious if a bit strong for my tastes.

"Excuse me, Miss," a voice said at my elbow. I turned in surprise and found the dark haired gentleman standing there. "Might I have the pleasure of knowing your name?"

I could not help my smile, but it was one of amusement as well as surprise. The gentlemen in London were far different than the ones in Hertfordshire. "Elizabeth Bennet," I said. "And you are?"

"Fitzwilliam Darcy," he replied with a small bow.

"I am very pleased to make your acquaintance, Mr. Darcy," I said, though I did not know what else I should say.

"The pleasure is mine, Miss Bennet."

We stood there for a moment, just looking at each other, and I felt an odd tension building between us. It was almost as if we were sizing each other up, trying to decide if we liked what we saw.

"I must confess," I said after a moment, "that I did not expect to find many interesting people at this ball."

"No?" he said, eyebrow raised.

"No," I laughed and then regretted my mirth at once. It was a nervous laughter, and I wondered if he had noticed. "I know none of the young ladies that I arrived with, and my aunt is the one who arranged my invitation... It does not help matters that most of the gentlemen here seem to be more interested in dancing than conversation, and the ladies are all too occupied with their own charms to give anyone else a second glance. I do not mind dancing, of course... but I find that I am—"

"Not in the mood?"

I nodded and took a sip of my punch and then grimaced at the taste.

"Lady Bearing is rather... heavy-handed with the rum," he said. "Her punch is famous for precisely that reason."

"I would have to agree," I choked out.

We were interrupted by the sound of someone clearing their throat behind us. We turned around and I saw a slender fair-haired gentleman watching us with a bemused expression upon his face.

"Ahem," he said. "Forgive me for interrupting, but I must steal Mr. Darcy away for a moment."

"Of course," I said with a smile. "I am sure we will have a chance to speak again, Mr. Darcy."

The gentleman seemed reluctant to leave me, and as he walked away with his friend he looked back over his shoulder at me and I was struck once again by the depths of his gaze.

As the two gentlemen retreated into the throng of guests, I found myself unable to shake the image of Mr. Darcy's enigmatic smile and the warmth that had flickered within his dark eyes. The brief encounter with him had stirred something within me—a curiosity, a longing, an indescribable yearning to know more about this mysterious gentleman who had so unexpectedly captured my attention.

"Miss Bennet," called out Miss Kelly, breaking into my thoughts with her excitable tone. "Are you quite well? You seem rather lost. Lady Bearing's punch can be rather... overbearing." She leaned close and lowered her voice, "much like her ladyship."

I laughed and smiled at her. "Ah, yes, I am well," I reassured her. "I was simply reflecting on an encounter just now."

"An encounter?" Miss Kelly's blue eyes sparkled with curiosity. "Do tell."

"Perhaps later," I replied, unwilling to share the details of my conversation with Mr. Darcy just yet. Especially with a stranger whose motives I did not know.

My thoughts lingered on him, and I tried to recall every detail of his visage—the chiseled lines of his jaw, the waves of his dark hair, and the way his eyes seemed to pierce through me, as if he could see straight into my soul.

"Very well," Miss Kelly conceded, a knowing smile playing at her lips. "But do join us in the dance. It is unbecoming to stand idly by while others enjoy themselves."

"Of course," I agreed, trying to push Mr. Darcy from my mind and focus on the present. As we joined the dance, however, I found myself glancing around the room, hoping to catch a glimpse of him amid the sea of swirling gowns and tailored coats.

As the evening wore on, I could not help but feel a growing sense of longing in my chest, a desire for the conversation that had been cut short between Mr. Darcy and myself. My thoughts were consumed by him—his enigmatic charm, and the depth of emotion that I had glimpsed beneath his guarded exterior.

And though I tried to convince myself that it was mere curiosity, deep within me stirred something far more powerful

—an attraction that both frightened and exhilarated me in equal measure. But it had been so brief—how could I place such meaning on so short an acquaintance?

The night dragged on, each passing moment feeling like an eternity as I searched the crowd for Mr. Darcy.

I continued to dance with any gentleman who asked, but my mind was far from the dance floor. I found myself drawn to the sidelines, gazing at the couples spinning around me with a sense of longing.

I longed for someone who could engage me in conversation, who could challenge me and make my heart race. I truly did wish for a connection that was more than just polite small talk or idle chatter.

But that was not to be found here.

In a moment of desperate pique I found my aunt talking with some of her friends near the banquet tables.

"Why, Lizzy, whatever is the matter?" she asked.

"I— Nothing," I said quickly, not wishing to worry her. I was fine, truly, I just could not be in the ballroom any longer. "I would like to return to Gracechurch Street, I think," I said. "My head—"

"Ah, yes. Of course, my dear," my aunt said with a kindly smile. She murmured an apology to her friends and wound her arm through mine to lead me toward the foyer of Lady Bearing's grand house.

"Are you well," she asked softly. "Truly?"

"I am, I promise," I replied. "The ball is just... overwhelming."

"These events can be so," my aunt agreed. She looked at me carefully. "But you do seem out of sorts. When you return to Gracechurch Street, ask Mrs. Wells for a tonic. She will know which one. It will help you sleep and chase away any headache that might be looming. Lady Bearing's punch is... potent."

"It is, indeed," I laughed. "Thank you again. Tonight was wonderful. Truly."

My aunt kissed my cheek and smoothed my hair back from my forehead. "I shall return very soon. Your uncle will not be waiting up for me so I feel no guilt in the matter."

Her smile was full of mischief and I could not help my laughter. "I shall say nothing at all," I promised.

"Good girl," my aunt said with a wink. "Now, go and find a carriage. We shall speak more in the morning... or perhaps at teatime."

"Teatime it shall be," I said. "Goodnight, aunt."

"Goodnight, my dear."

I walked out of the foyer with my shoulders back and my head held high, but I did hope that Mr. Darcy would somehow appear out of the crowd to speak with me again... But he did not, and I found a carriage that would take me back to Gracechurch Street in short order.

On the short journey from Bearing House I had time to ponder my interaction with the enigmatic gentleman... I knew nothing about him. Did not know where he was from or who his family might be. I only knew that he was handsome, and that I had enjoyed his company. I scolded myself for being so distracted by that one interrupted interaction that I had paid almost no attention to the other gentlemen who had demanded my attention that evening. I had danced with the son of an earl, a captain in the King's navy, and several other notable gentlemen... but I recalled nothing else about them.

I did not even know if I had enjoyed their company.

Mr. Darcy had been the only one in my thoughts.

"You are a fool, Elizabeth Bennet," I whispered.

I was a fool. I had allowed my desperation to get the best of me. But I could not wallow in such things forever.

I had come to London to escape my mother, but I had also

come to London to break the monotony of my routine. I knew that I should write to Charlotte. It had already been too long between her wedding and our last correspondence, and I began to worry that she would think I was angry with her.

I was not, of course. But she could not know that.

When the carriage arrived at Gracechurch Street, I thanked the driver and climbed the stairs to the front door of the Gardiner's house with a heavy heart.

My uncle's valet opened the door and welcomed me with hushed tones before pointing to the open door of the drawing room.

I peered into the room and smiled as I saw my uncle, snoring in his chair by the fire with an open book in his lap.

"He was waiting for Mrs. Gardiner," the valet murmured.

"Very sweet of him," I said with a smile. "My aunt will not be returning until the ball has ended."

The man nodded and I bid him goodnight and climbed the stairs toward the bedchamber I had been given for my stay in London. Not for the first time I wished that Jane had accompanied me. I longed to speak with her about the ball and what had happened there—she would know what to say and how to set my mind at ease.

She always knew what to say.

I rang for some washing water and the tonic that my aunt had mentioned. While I did not have a headache, I would be grateful for sleep... As I changed out of the beautiful gown I had been lent for the ball I thought again of Mr. Fitzwilliam Darcy.

What would I do if I were to see him again? What would I say to him? Or he to me?

Would he apologize for being pulled away from our conversation? Or would he speak to me and enquire about my health without mentioning his friend's poorly timed intrusion?

Or had it been purposefully timed?

That thought had not occurred to me previously. What if the fair-haired gentleman was saving his friend from an imprudent match? I was certainly not of the same society as the other young ladies in attendance—but he could not have known that. Could he?

I swallowed a sudden anger that flared in my chest. "A coincidence, surely," I murmured.

Do not be so hasty in your judgments.

That was what Jane would say to me... but I had yet to be proven wrong.

As I dressed for bed and braided my hair, I resolved to write to Charlotte. A visit was overdue. I had to swallow my wounded pride and face Mr. Collins. I would, after all, have to face him when my father died and advocate on behalf of my mother and unmarried sisters to be sure that we would receive the care and be treated with the dignity we deserved.

I sipped the warm tonic that had been brought upstairs for me and pulled a fresh sheet of paper from my writing desk. First, a letter to Jane to tell her of my plans, and then I would write to Charlotte and hope that she would forgive me for being so negligent in my correspondence.

three

CHARLOTTE'S REPLY to my letter had been more enthusiastic than I could have hoped, and her invitation to visit Hunsford, while unexpected, was something that I had been reluctant to suggest, but I knew that it was my duty to speak to Mr. Collins. As much as I hated the idea of it, it was necessary. I was, however, unsure of how I would be received. Nevertheless, I knew in my heart that it was something I needed to do.

A fortnight had passed since Lady Bearing's ball, and, as I had hoped, the frequency that Mr. Darcy appeared in my thoughts had lessened considerably.

"Lizzy, I am sad to see you go," my aunt said as I prepared for my departure. "I had hoped that you would be able to accompany me to another society event—"

The hope that I might see Mr. Darcy again flared in my chest, but I forced myself to shake my head. "I am long overdue to visit my dear Charlotte," I said. "But perhaps on my return I will be able to do so."

"Are you certain that you are ready to face Mr. Collins?"

I was not certain, at all, but I had already wasted far too much time.

"It is necessary," I said. "I have a duty to my family, as well as to my friend, and I have ignored both for far too long."

"You do not have to be so cruel to yourself, Lizzy," my aunt said gently. "There is time—"

"I know," I said. "But I have been reminded of my own responsibilities, and I should not put them off."

My aunt nodded but I could feel her trepidation as she embraced me. Thankfully, the arrival of the carriage prevented any additional admonishments, and I was almost grateful to pick up my valise and walk down the stairs to the street.

"Write to me when you arrive at Hunsford," my aunt called after me.

"I shall, I promise," I called back. "I shall not stay long in Kent."

Mrs. Gardiner waved as I settled myself in the carriage and the footman closed the door behind me and I smiled back at her.

My aunt was one of my most cherished relatives, but I could not bear her pity.

THE CARRIAGE JOSTLED over the uneven country roads, my thoughts as disordered as the landscape that passed me by. Hunsford approached, and with it, the tangled web of emotions that accompanied my decision to visit Charlotte in her new life as Mrs. Collins.

Though I had been resolute in my refusal of Mr. Collins' proposal, a gnawing guilt lingered at the edges of my conscience.

Would not the securing of my family's future be worth the sacrifice of happiness? Was I selfish for valuing my own autonomy above my sisters' hopes and their security?

"Miss Bennet," the driver called out as we halted in front of the parsonage, snapping me from my reverie. "We have arrived."

"Thank you," I replied, gathering my belongings and stepping out into the brisk air.

The sight of the modest parsonage did little to dispel the heaviness in my chest. The door had been freshly painted in a deep green color that I knew Charlotte disliked immensely. I wondered if I would have been given the choice of color if I had become Mrs. Collins, or if Lady Catherine's choice would also have been taken into account.

Perhaps her ladyship's preference was the only option presented.

The small fence was also freshly painted and I admired the arrangement of the gardens that followed the stone path that led to the front door.

The dark green door opened as the carriage pulled away and Charlotte stepped out into the afternoon sun. "Elizabeth!" My friend's smile was warm but tired. "How wonderful to see you again!"

"Charlotte, my dear, I do hope that you can forgive me for staying away for so long," I said as I embraced her. Despite my conflicting feelings about her marriage, she remained one of my dearest confidantes. "It is truly a pleasure to see you."

"Please, you must come inside. You must be exhausted— It will only take a moment to put on some tea." As we walked through the narrow hallway, I could not help but note the strained atmosphere that pervaded the house.

"Mr. Collins will join us shortly," Charlotte informed me. "He is... quite eager to see you again."

"Ah, yes," I murmured, my stomach twisting into knots.

Charlotte led me into a bright parlor where a small fire burned in the small hearth to keep the chill out of the room. The furnishings were sparse and well-worn, and I wondered what kind of salary Mr. Collins was afforded by his patroness. It would have been understandable that a bachelor would not care so much for the furnishings in his parlor, but now that Charlotte was here—

"Charlotte— How are you?" I asked as I sank down into one of the chairs that had been arranged near the fire.

Charlotte perched on the edge of the chair opposite me, clearly distracted by a noise in the corridor.

"I beg your pardon?"

"Are you well?" I asked again.

"Oh, yes," she replied. "Very well." But her smile seemed forced.

"Are you happy here? The parsonage is very— quaint."

"It is a good deal smaller than Lucas Lodge, to be sure," Charlotte said. "But that was to be expected. It is not practical for a parson to have a large house. Mr. Collins has spoken of it at length. Lady Catherine believes that there should be enough room for the beginnings of a small family, but that I should not expect the extravagance of my former life."

"Indeed not," I murmured.

It was then that Mr. Collins entered the drawing room, his face flushed with excitement.

"Miss Bennet, what an honor it is to welcome you into our humble abode!" His exaggerated bow sent a shiver down my spine, a stark reminder of the life I could have led. "My dear Charlotte and I could not be happier in our union, and we are most delighted to share our happiness with you."

"Thank you, Mr. Collins," I replied, forcing a polite smile. "I am glad to hear that you are both content." My eyes flickered to Charlotte, who did not quite meet my gaze.

"Indeed! We have been truly blessed by Providence," he continued, oblivious to the tension in the room. "And it is my fervent desire that you, too, will find such happiness one day."

"Your sentiments are most kind," I managed, swallowing the lump in my throat. As the conversation meandered through trivial matters, I found myself unable to shake the disquiet that had settled upon me. Charlotte had made this choice out of practicality... but I could not help but wonder if my own life would have been the same if I had made the same decision.

As the tea arrived, I noticed Mr. Collins' eyes lingered on me for a moment too long, his gaze intense. I shifted uncomfortably in my seat and focused on stirring my tea. To my relief, Charlotte began to speak of her new acquaintances in Kent, including the esteemed Lady Catherine De Bourgh.

"Lady Catherine is one of the most respected ladies in all of Kent," Mr. Collins interrupted fervently. "Her opinions are greatly valued by all who know her."

"Indeed," I murmured politely, but my thoughts wandered to the rumors I had heard about Lady Catherine's domineering personality. Mr. Collins was, of course, nothing but complimentary toward his patroness, which I had expected, and his esteem of her was suffocating.

I could not imagine living under Lady Catherine's watchful eye.

As the conversation turned to more benign topics, I began to relax slightly. But a sudden realization struck me—

It was painfully clear that Charlotte was unhappy. Despite her brave words regarding practicality and contentment, there was an emptiness in her eyes that spoke of disappointment and resignation.

I knew that I should speak to her privately about her true feelings, but I did not know if I would be able to find such an opportunity. If Mr. Collins persisted in his need to hover over every conversation, I would have to take matters into my own hands.

. . .

THE FOLLOWING MORNING, I rose early and washed my face with the cold water left in the wash basin from the night before. I dressed carefully, and as quietly as possible so as not to wake anyone else in the house.

But as I went downstairs, I could hear Mr. Collins moving around on the main floor, pacing his study and talking to himself in agitated tones behind the closed door of his study. I could only imagine that he was practicing his upcoming sermon—perhaps preparing to present it to Lady Catherine de Bourgh over tea.

I pressed myself against the wall of the corridor that led to the kitchens as the door to Mr. Collins' study opened and his heavy footsteps echoed on the carpeted floor. I crept into the kitchen, careful not to let the door make any noise as it closed behind me.

Pressing my ear to the wooden door I listened to Mr. Collins' footsteps as he walked through the house, and flinched as the front door slammed shut.

I rushed to the small window to watch the parson as he walked with purposeful steps to the path that I could only assume led to Rosings Park and his beloved patroness who was most likely, despite the earliness of the hour, expecting his arrival.

The Collins' had not been given a cook, as Charlotte had told me, and Mr. Collins had confirmed, Lady Catherine expected that it was the wifely duty to be a useful sort of person in all aspects of the household. I did not think that Charlotte could cook, but I had not been able to ask her. According to Mr. Collins, a cook would be sent down to the parsonage only once per day to prepare supper and instruct Charlotte on how best to manage in the kitchens.

As far as I could recall, Charlotte could make a passable pot of tea, but if the scones I had attempted to eat upon my arrival at the parsonage the day before, the instruction was not progressing as well as one might hope.

"You would have been miserable, too," I murmured as I re-stoked the fire in the hearth and set the kettle over it to boil.

I was not useless in the kitchen, but Mrs. Hill did not allow us to assist her with the preparation of meals or anything more complicated than arranging a tray of biscuits for tea. I could not imagine what it would be like to be thrust into a life without the assistance of any servants. Lucas Lodge was teeming with maids, footmen, a housekeeper, a butler, and a valet... I could not imagine how full the kitchen would be with all of the scullery maids and kitchen helpers as well as the cooks who watched over everything.

With Mr. Collins out of the house, I would have time to speak to Charlotte—but in truth I wished only to be alone.

After drinking a hastily prepared cup of tea, I went quietly back up to my bedchamber, took a book from my valise, and laid a wool blanket over my arm. With the intent of reading in the early morning sunshine, I cast a look over my shoulder down the corridor toward Charlotte's room and wondered if I should wake her.

But I reasoned that she would appreciate some peace and quiet, especially with Mr. Collins gone. I would be able to speak to her later, of that I was certain.

I left the house as quietly as possible and ignored the growling of my stomach as I walked along the path.

It did not take me long to find the apple orchard that Mr. Collins had spoken of so proudly—according to my cousin, Lady Catherine was very fond of the apples that came from these trees, and would have no others when it came to her spiced apple cider, her stewed apple tarts, or, indeed, the apple sauce that graced the holiday table at Rosings Park.

To my eye they looked like any other apple tree and I shook

my head as I entered the lines of trees and looked for a sturdy one to lean against as I read.

As I settled against my chosen tree, I regarded the parsonage carefully. It seemed a quaint place to make a life for oneself—if Mr. Collins were not part of the picture that was painted. I looked over my shoulder at the looming shadow of Rosings Park. The great house was perched upon the hill like a great bird of prey, and the windows that Mr. Collins spoke of with such reverence glittered in the sunlight and reminded me of eyes—ever watchful of what happened on the estate below.

A shiver ran up my spine at the thought of never being able to escape Lady Catherine's scrutiny and I reminded myself once more that I had made the right decision.

Just the sight of Mr. Collins' face and the sanctimonious tone of his voice had been enough to confirm my initial reactions to him. But the threat of Lady Catherine's ever-present judgment would have been too much to bear. My mother would have to understand. Some day, perhaps.

I shook my head and opened my book, but I was not able to read more than a few paragraphs before I heard a voice.

"Oh no, please let it not be Mr. Collins," I muttered. I held my breath, hoping that whoever it was would move on, but they did not. The voice grew louder as they approached—a gentleman.

four

I ROSE TO MY FEET, suddenly alarmed, and tucked my book under my arm just in case I needed a weapon to fend off a dangerous—

No. That was ridiculous.

I cleared my throat and called out to the stranger who I could not see through the trees. "Hello? Who is there?"

I peered through the leaves, and finally spotted a gentleman. "Hello?" I called again.

My shout had clearly caught the gentleman by surprise, and as he turned to look in my direction, his boot slipped on the wet grass and sent him sprawling onto the ground at the foot of the apple tree.

I struggled to muffle the laughter that burst forth from my lips at the gentleman's unceremonious fall, and I choked on it as he struggled to get to his feet once more. A patch of green streaked the beige fabric of his fine breeches and marred his coat, and his glossy boots were caked with mud.

"Unbelievable," he muttered as he brushed at the grass stains on his coat.

"Are you quite all right?" I asked.

"No thanks to you," he snapped. "If you had not startled me—"

Taken aback, I strode through the trees toward him. "I beg your pardon," I said. "I was not aware that anyone else would be out walking, otherwise I would have avoided this area. But I was here first, and it is *you* who have intruded upon my solitude."

"I did not see you—"

I pushed aside the bough of an apple tree and stepped into the gentleman's view. But as soon as I saw his face, my angry retort died in my throat.

Mr. Fitzwilliam Darcy.

"What are you doing here?" he blurted out.

I met his incredulous gaze boldly.

"I should ask you the same thing," I said. "I was reading under a tree. What are *you* doing here?"

He glanced at the book that was under my arm and then met my eyes once more. He seemed embarrassed to be caught in the wrong.

Good.

"I— I am walking— That is not what I meant!"

I tried not to smile, but it was almost impossible. He was ridiculously easy to tease.

"I did not think that I would see you again after the ball," he said.

"Nor did I. You departed my company in such a hurry that I despaired that I had done something to offend you."

The gentleman shook his head. "No, indeed," he said with a chuckle. "Far from it."

His dark hair was unruly and his dark eyes held mine with an intensity that took my breath away. I had certainly embarrassed him... and then teased him for it. And still he wished to speak to me. How could—

"Mr. Darcy—"

"Yes?"

"What are you doing here? In Hunsford? Do you not live in London?"

He seemed flustered, but only for a moment. "No, indeed, I do not. My estate is in Derbyshire. Not far from here, to be sure, but far enough." He smiled, but it was crooked and disarming. "Rosings Park belongs to my aunt, Lady Catherine de Bourgh."

"Ah," I said with a grimace before I could stop myself. "I have heard *all* about her Ladyship from my cousin."

"Your cousin?"

"Mr. Collins," I said. "He is the parson here..."

"Indeed he is," Mr. Darcy said with some chagrin.

Oh, dear.

A silence fell between us. I was torn between two emotions —elation at seeing him once more, and a distinct feeling of embarrassment that I had remained so fixated upon him for the last fortnight without knowing anything about him. I had not even enquired after him...

But what happened now?

His eyes brightened just a little, but it might have been my imagination. "Miss Bennet, I must ask you something—"

"Yes, Mr. Darcy?"

"Will you—"

"Cousin! Cousin Elizabeth! Are you here?"

I could not help my frown as I recognized Mr. Collins' voice.

"My cousin," I muttered. "Always arriving where he is least welcome." I forced a smile onto my face and turned in the direction of the intruding voice. "I am here, Mr. Collins," I called out, though I did not wish to see him at all.

The parson cursed under his breath as he pushed through

the branches and I pressed my fingers to my lips to keep from laughing as the portly man stumbled through the wet grass.

"My dear Charlotte has asked me to come and find you," he puffed. "It seems that we may be dining at Rosing Park tomorrow night, and I should like to prepare you to meet her Ladyship—"

The parson stopped dead in his tracks as he laid eyes upon me.

"Mr. Collins, I trust that you are already acquainted with Mr. Darcy," I said with a smile.

"We are, indeed," Mr. Collins stammered. "Mr. Darcy, I am surprised to see you here. I was lately at Pemberley—"

"I know," he said somewhat stiffly. "I was called away on business to London."

"Indeed," Mr. Collins said. His mannerisms repulsed me, and I struggled to keep my expression neutral when all I wished to do was run in the opposite direction.

"Cousin, if you please—"

"Will you be at Rosings Park for very long," I asked the gentleman suddenly.

"I will, indeed, be in attendance for the next fortnight," he replied.

"Wonderful. Perhaps I shall see you again, Mr. Darcy."

"Perhaps," he murmured.

As Mr. Collins led me away toward the parsonage, I noticed him glance over his shoulder at the gentleman we left behind. I could not bring myself to do the same. Though I was thrilled to see him again, I was preoccupied with other confusions... not to mention that we had been invited to supper at Rosings Park, and from Mr. Collins' mannerisms, I could already see that this would be an important affair. At least in his estimations.

Back at the parsonage, my thoughts were consumed by Mr. Darcy's unexpected appearance in Hunsford. Why had our paths crossed once more? My heart ached with the weight of unresolved emotions, and I struggled to focus on Mr. Collins' prattling as we took tea in the parlor.

Charlotte had made a fresh batch of scones which were, admittedly, better than the last, but still unpalatable without a hefty helping of jam to distract from their dryness.

"Cousin Elizabeth," Mr. Collins finally announced, drawing my attention back to the present, "as I mentioned before, we have been invited to Rosings Park for supper tomorrow evening. Lady Catherine has heard of your presence in Hunsford and wishes to make your acquaintance."

"Indeed?" I replied, unable to conceal my trepidation. The prospect of meeting the formidable Lady Catherine de Bourgh was daunting enough, but to do so under the watchful eye of Mr. Darcy left me feeling utterly exposed.

"Her ladyship expects nothing less than perfect decorum," Mr. Collins warned, his brow furrowed in disapproval. "She is particularly fond of discussing the accomplishments of young ladies. You would do well to prepare yourself accordingly."

"Thank you for the advice, Mr. Collins," I murmured, my mind still preoccupied with thoughts of Mr. Darcy. Would our reunion provide closure, or only serve to further complicate matters between us? A thousand questions swirled through my head, leaving me more confused than ever.

* * *

AFTER AN AWKWARD SUPPER, I lay awake for several hours listening to the settling of the parsonage. The creaks and groans of the wood were comforting, but I did not feel at home in that place. Once again, I told myself that my decision to refuse Mr. Collins' suit had been the correct one.

But I did not allow myself to think anything of the fact that Mr. Darcy had somehow reappeared in my sphere.

It was a coincidence only. Nothing more.

But even though that was my last thought before sleep overtook me, when I awoke before dawn the following morning, I could not shake the image of him from my mind.

I washed my face with cold water once more, dressed quickly, and snuck downstairs to the kitchens to make myself a cup of tea. The house was silent, and I did not think that Mr. Collins had risen yet.

If I was to avoid him for as long as possible, I would have to find something to keep me busy. I noticed the basket of scones that Charlotte had made and grimaced as I remembered their taste. Too dry, and with too much salt. Perhaps I could make an attempt at the recipe the cook from Rosings Park had left behind.

I worked diligently to complete the recipe and make the least amount of noise possible, and when I was finally able to remove them from the oven I was pleasantly surprised to see that they looked a good deal more palatable than I had expected. Perhaps even Mrs. Hill would be proud of my efforts if she had been here to see them.

"Wonderful," I murmured as I broke off the piece of one small scone as a reward for my efforts. It did not taste as good as I recalled Mrs. Hill's scones tasting, but it was a far cry from the dry cakes that Charlotte had made. I tucked my offerings into a basket and covered them with a piece of linen before setting the basket beside the teapot I had prepared.

I hoped that Charlotte would not take offense to my assistance. But now that my task was done, I was desperate to leave the warmth of the kitchen and walk in the fresh morning air.

I pulled my shawl over my shoulders, brushed the flour

from my cheek, and set off toward the foyer. I pulled open the front door and almost let out a scream of surprise as a fist came toward my face.

"Miss Bennet," the gentleman choked out.

"Mr. Darcy," I exclaimed, equally surprised as I realized who was standing on the step. "Good morning— What brings you to the parsonage?"

"I—"

"I was just about to take a walk," I continued briskly. There was no time for embarrassment, and I did not wish to draw any attention to myself or run the risk that Mr. Collins would come downstairs and ruin this moment. Which he undoubtedly would. "Would you like to— join me?"

The question was bold. He stared at me in surprise for a moment.

"Unless you are here to speak with Mr. Collins?" I asked, at once a little surprised by my own words.

"No, indeed," he said hastily. "I actually... I came here to speak to you, Miss Bennet."

"To... me?"

"Indeed."

I lifted my chin and stepped over the threshold, pulling the parsonage door closed behind me. "Then we shall walk," I said briskly. "Come along, Mr. Darcy."

I strode past him with my head held high, unwilling to let him see how out of my depth I really was.

I did not slow my pace, even though I knew that I should have. Young ladies of proper breeding and character did not walk like boys... but I did not wish to dawdle for the sake of propriety.

"Miss Bennet, may I ask," he blurted out as he caught up with me. "Where is your family from?"

"Hertfordshire," I replied briskly.

He paused. "Not from London?"

"Certainly not," I scoffed. "My father has not stepped one foot in London in almost thirty years and, much to my mother's chagrin, he is *very* proud of that fact."

"Indeed."

His pause was longer this time and I wondered if I had said too much.

"Are you enquiring after my family's society, Mr. Darcy?" I asked without turning around to look at him.

"I—"

I was certain that was his aim, although his approach was clumsy.

"I must admit that I was out of my element at Lady Bearing's ball," I said. "But I could not find a sound enough excuse to stay home. My aunt was quite insistent on my attendance."

"I am glad of it," he said.

My cheeks warmed slightly, and I hoped that he could not tell. "We spoke for such a short time," I said. "I daresay you would have been grateful that your time was not wasted on me. I do hope that the young lady you spoke with after me was from a better sort of society?"

I was teasing him again, and thankfully he seemed to notice before I felt the need to apologize and explain myself again.

"She was... not what I had hoped," he admitted with some chagrin.

"A pity."

"Indeed."

We walked in silence for a few moments before he spoke again. "Miss Bennet, I must apologize for my behavior at the ball. I should not have left so abruptly without explanation."

"It is of no consequence, Mr. Darcy," I said with a wave of my hand. "I am sure you had your reasons."

"I did," he replied, "but they were not sufficient to justify my rudeness."

I looked at him then, studying his face for a moment before I spoke. "Very well, your apology is acceptable, Mr. Darcy."

He breathed a sigh of relief. "Thank you, Miss Bennet." He paused again, and I could not be certain what it was that was giving him so much difficulty...

"There was something else I wished to discuss with you," he blurted out.

"Oh?"

"I find myself in a bit of a predicament."

"Pray, tell me what it is," I said with a genuine concern that was unexpected.

He hesitated once more, and I found myself wondering if I should be nervous about what he might have to say.

"I am engaged—" he blurted out, "well, not really engaged — but my aunt believes it to be so," he finished, his voice barely above a whisper.

I stared at him in surprise. "Engaged, but that is wonderful." And then I narrowed my eyes at him. "But... I am confused."

"It is a falsehood," he said. "A fiction..."

I stopped walking and shook my head in confusion. "A fiction?"

He nodded.

"How did this come about?"

"I—" He swallowed hard, obviously nervous. But what reason would a gentleman such as he have to be nervous?

All at once he let out a quick breath and said, "I used your likeness in a portrait to convince her."

He had—

"I beg your pardon?" My words were sharp and clipped.

"I— It is as I have said—"

"You used *my* likeness to— pretend to an engagement," I said vehemently. "How— How could you do such a thing?"

"I—"

He seemed taken aback by my fury, but I could not contain my anger. *How dare he do such a thing!*

five

"I CAN EXPLAIN—"

"No, Mr. Darcy," I interrupted, my voice cold. "I do not think you can." I turned on my heel and began to walk away from him, shaking my head in disbelief. I wanted to scream with rage and throw something. But I could do neither of those things.

"Miss Bennet, please," he said, but I did not turn to look at him. "I know that what I did was inexcusable and unforgivable but I beg of you to hear me out."

I stopped abruptly and spun around to glare at him. "And why should I do that, Mr. Darcy? Why should I listen to a man who disregards a woman's feelings and uses her likeness without permission for his own selfish gain?"

"I have no excuse," he said softly, taking a step closer.

"And what was your plan, precisely, in using a portrait of me to aid in your deception?" I snapped.

"I was desperate to please my aunt and turn her attention away from my life so that I could focus on the estate and my own business pursuits. She has been watching me far too carefully since my father died..."

I folded her arms over my chest as I glared at him. That was not the answer I had been expecting. Nor was it a suitable explanation.

"I had intended to show my aunt the portrait, and then—"

"And then what? Continue on with your life as though nothing had happened and wait for her to forget that you had never married?"

"I— essentially... yes."

"And now you have been caught in your own deceptions," I said, suddenly realizing what must have happened.

He nodded grimly. "My aunt wishes to meet you—"

"Me?" I cried. "You have used my *name* as *well* as my likeness?"

"It was a mistake—"

"Indeed it was," I fumed. "How *easy* it must be to be a man and not have to wonder what a shambles your reputation would be after the ruse was played out. You simply intended to... not speak of it any longer? Or, perhaps, you would craft another lie about how I had *died* suddenly— Or, disappeared to the colonies or the continent! What *bliss* to be so free."

I did not bother to rein in my anger. He deserved every bit of my ire, and from the look on his face, he knew it, too.

"Miss Bennet, you are right," he said finally.

I stared at him in disbelief.

"You... agree with me?"

"I do," he said. "Using your likeness was my first mistake, and I did think that my deception would not be challenged, or discovered. It was wrong of me to use you in such a way and I am deeply sorry."

"An apology made in an apple orchard does not undo what you have done," I said firmly. I could feel my heart pounding against my ribs. I felt ill and furious—exploding into a column of flames would have been preferable at that moment to anything else.

"I know," he replied. "But, please, Miss Bennet, allow me the opportunity to make it up to you. Allow me to show you that I am not the man you believe me to be."

He regarded me silently for a moment, weighing the options that had been set before me. I could see no way to undo what had been done... I needed to know everything.

To his credit, the gentleman waited patiently for me to come to a decision.

Finally I nodded in agreement. "Very well," I said. "But it will take more than mere words for me to forgive you. And the threat to my own reputation is... It is not something to be taken lightly. I might be just the daughter of a country gentleman, but if word of this were to reach Hertfordshire—or my aunt's family in London..."

"I promise that it will not leave Rosings Park," he said.

"And who else knows about this deception?"

"I— My closest friend, Charles Bingley in London."

I frowned. "I see."

"But no one else."

Impossible.

"The painter? How did he manage to paint my likeness if I did not sit for the portrait? Does it even look like me?"

The gentleman pulled a small velvet-wrapped package out of my jacket pocket and held it out to me. I snatched it out of his hand and unwrapped it without hesitation, and I could not help the way my breath caught as I looked at it.

The portrait was... me. As though I were looking in a mirror.

"Goodness—" I whispered.

"I described you to the painter," he said in a rush.

"Indeed," I muttered, trying my best not to show how much I had been shaken by the likeness he had commissioned of me. He had described me... precisely, in such detail. Why— How could he have...

I pushed those thoughts away. I was angry. I was angry with him for what he had done. This was not the time to forget why this had been painted in the first place.

"Now, what did you want—" I demanded. "Did you come here just to interrupt my walk and confront me with your deceptions?"

"I— No, that is... Miss Bennet, I need your help."

"My *help*?" My laughter echoed in the early morning and the gentleman flinched at it.

Good.

He deserved to be uncomfortable.

"Yes. My aunt has expressed her wish to meet you."

I stared at him. "She has?"

"She has demanded it, actually," he said.

"I see. And you would wish for me to come to Rosings Park for supper, as has already been planned, *not* as a guest of my cousin Mr. Collins, but as the woman you are engaged to."

"Yes."

"Which means that I shall have to tell my cousin, and his new wife."

He nodded, his expression strained. "It would seem prudent to do so."

"Indeed, else there would be a great surprise at supper."

I kept my tone sharp and my glare in place as I re-wrapped the portrait and tucked it into a pocket in my skirts.

"My good friend Charlotte, who has just recently become Mrs. Collins, is the daughter of one of the most notorious gossips in all of Hertfordshire," I said as I folded my hands at my waist in an attempt to focus more completely on the problem at hand. "She will, of course, tell her mother about this happy news... Which means that by the time I return home the entirety of Hertfordshire society will know about it."

The gentleman seemed to understand the weight of the

situation then. This little ruse would affect me far more than it would him. He could retire to his estate and deny that any of it had ever happened—but I... I could not be so cavalier.

"I understand your concern, Miss Bennet, but I promise you that I will do everything in my power to ensure that our engagement remains a private matter until we can determine the best way to move forward."

"The best way to keep it from ruining everything," I said sharply. I looked at him for a long moment before finally nodding. "Very well, Mr. Darcy. I shall agree to meet Lady Catherine de Bourgh, and I shall play along with your charade for the time being, but make no mistake: I shall not stand for any more deceptions. I will speak to Charlotte and tell her to keep her counsel on this matter."

"I understand," he said with some relief. "Thank you, Miss Bennet."

"Save your gratitude," I said as I turned away. "We shall see what happens at supper."

* * *

THE GRAND ENTRANCE of Rosings Park loomed before me, its magnificent facade adorned with meticulously carved columns and intricate stonework. The perfectly mani-cured gardens sprawled across the vast estate, interwoven with sinuous gravel paths that led to dazzling fountains and rose-covered trellises. It was a world apart from the modest comforts of Longbourn, and I felt the weight of my decision as I stood at the threshold.

I had agreed to accompany Mr. Darcy to this dinner under the pretense of our "engagement" – an arrangement born of necessity rather than romance. Lady Catherine de Bourgh, Mr. Darcy's formidable aunt, demanded to meet and approve of me as a potential match for her beloved nephew. My heart raced as I contemplated the challenges that lay ahead, but I steeled myself, determined to help Mr. Darcy maintain the facade for the sake of his reputation and the future of our families.

The stone-faced butler who opened the front door of Rosings Park barely acknowledged Mr. Collins' effusive greeting before he led us down the corridor toward the parlor.

The room was grander than anything I had ever been in before, grander even than Lucas Lodge, and it was difficult to know where to look. However opulent it was, the room was chilly, and I wished that I could have brought my shawl, but Mr. Collins had insisted that it was not necessary. I envied him for his woolen frock coat.

Lady Catherine had not yet arrived, which I had expected. A woman such as her ladyship would likely enjoy making an entrance to impress her guests. She would not have seen any harm in keeping us waiting.

As we stood in the parlor, unable to sit without her Lady-ship's permission, Mr. Collins tested me on topics of conversation and reminded me of which things I would be permitted to say. I was not to have too many opinions, and I was not to question anything her ladyship said in any way.

A dreary prospect, and a promise that I was not certain I would be able to maintain.

Finally, just when I thought I might ask for Charlotte's sake, Mr. Collins muttered something about sitting. Charlotte walked immediately toward the window and perched on the edge of a thin gilt chair. I did the same, grateful to be seated, if only for a moment.

Charlotte said nothing, she had been stunned by the announcement of the engagement as I had told her and Mr. Collins, and then immediately requested their discretion regarding the matter. I wondered if she was angry with me for not telling her sooner... but it was not as though I could have done so. But I could not explain that, either.

There was a small commotion in the corridor, and the shout of a command from an older woman before a wide-eyed footman entered the room and announced Lady Catherine de Bourgh's arrival.

Mr. Collins immediately swept into a deep bow, and Charlotte and I struggled to rise to our feet as her Ladyship entered the room.

Mr. Darcy followed behind his aunt, but I could not meet his gaze.

"Mr. Darcy," Mr. Collins cried. "How good it is to see you again."

"Indeed," the gentleman replied with a smile that I knew was forced.

Without preamble, Lady Catherine launched into a discussion with Charlotte about the planting of the kitchen garden just outside the parsonage. Lady Catherine, very obviously, prided herself on overseeing many aspects of the lives that were touched by her patronage... and as far as I could see that extended to a great many things.

I could feel Mr. Darcy's eyes upon me, but I could not bring myself to look at him. I knew that he would be wondering what decision I had made, and whether I would, indeed, honor my agreement to play along with the ruse he had crafted.

I could have left him to weather his aunt's wrath and felt no guilt for it.

But the more I had thought about it, the more I knew that I could do no such thing.

"Miss Bennet," Lady Catherine called out suddenly, her voice unnecessarily loud in the closeness of the parlor. "I have just been told of the wonderful news. An engagement! I had almost given up hope that my dear nephew would find a young lady who was worthy of our family."

All eyes turned to me and silence fell over the room. I held my breath as I glanced at Mr. Darcy and then back to Lady Catherine.

"Indeed, your Ladyship," I said with a smooth smile. "It was all very sudden. Your nephew is very... charming."

"It must be such an honor for you to be engaged to such a wealthy and distinguished gentleman as my Fitzwilliam," Lady Catherine said with an expectant smile.

"I consider myself fortunate to have found some happiness in this world when so many are denied it," I said evenly.

Lady Catherine's mouth twisted briefly and I wondered what she was thinking. "Indeed. Now, tell me, Miss Bennet. Your family—"

Lady Catherine paused, waiting for me to answer, but I could not decide how best to approach the situation, or what question she might be asking... I could only guess at what she would be expecting to hear.

The older woman's thin lips pressed into an even thinner line and I took a breath to force myself to speak.

"I have four sisters," I said finally.

"All out in society? Before the eldest are married?"

"Yes," she replied. "It is a practicality. My youngest sister is not yet sixteen. But they are all out— I do not think there is anything that could keep Lydia at home when there is a ball or a dance."

Lady Catherine's brows knitted briefly. I knew that there was a very specific way of doing things in the upper circles of society, but we could not entertain such luxuries.

"Then you do not reside in London?" she pressed.

"Indeed, I do not," I said. "Mr. Collins must have made you aware of my family's situation?"

Mr. Collins stepped forward, his hands already clutching nervously at the lapels of his black woolen jacket. "Your Ladyship will recall that I have spoken of Longbourn—"

Lady Catherine's chin rose slightly as she regarded the parson. "Only insofar as that you will inherit it when your cousin passes on— An entailment?"

"Indeed, your Ladyship," he simpered. "Your memory is, as always, perfect on this subject."

"Of course it is," Lady Catherine snapped. "Now, Miss Bennet. If you do not live in London, how is it that you met my nephew?"

"By chance, your Ladyship," I replied. "At Lady Bearing's ball in London. One that I had no intention of attending—and yet, it would seem that I was meant to be there."

Lady Catherine's smile was tight. It was clear enough to me that she did not believe in such romantic notions. "How wonderful. Fitzwilliam has never mentioned you before—"

"Indeed, he would not have been able to. Our courtship was... unexpectedly swift."

Lady Catherine turned slowly to look at her nephew, but Mr. Darcy said nothing, he merely inclined my head in agreement and I was grateful that he did not say anything to ruin what I had begun.

The stone-faced butler appeared in the doorway, but Lady Catherine did not wait for him to announce that it was time to move into the dining room.

She rose from her seat and fixed her imperious gaze upon me.

"You will sit near me," she said. "If I am to call you niece, I should like to know more about you. How large is your household—"

I took a deep breath and fell into step beside Lady Catherine.

"With five daughters, it is a... chaotic household," I said. "My father is a capable gentleman and managed his finances well, and the affairs of the tenants are all taken care of quite adeptly."

"I see," Lady Catherine mused. "And how many tenants?"

"Four, I believe," I said. "Enough to keep the household in good repair, and afford an education and care for my sisters and I—"

"Indeed," she said. "You are most intriguing, Miss Bennet. I should like to know more about you as we enjoy our supper."

"Thank you, your Ladyship," I murmured.

I could not allow myself to feel any relief... not yet.

This was only the beginning of the evening, and there was still time for everything to go very wrong.

six

THE TABLE WAS SET with fine gilded china and silverware that put anything my mother would set upon our table to shame, and I could only imagine the feast that awaited us that evening.

Her Ladyship took what must have been her usual seat at the head of the table, with Mr. Darcy and I flanking her on either side. Mr. Collins seemed somewhat perturbed and I wondered if I had taken his seat. He looked discomfited by the whole affair, but there was nothing he could say about it.

Dinner was served but I could barely eat anything; my nerves were frayed within an inch of breaking and I had to force myself not to stare at Mr. Darcy as he sat across the table from me.

Lady Catherine seemed to be enjoying herself immensely as she regaled her guests with tales of her latest charitable endeavors and gossip about the neighbors. I was trying her best to keep up with the conversation, but Lady Catherine did not seem to wish for a conversation, indeed her sharp tongue and imperious attitude made it difficult for anyone to get a word in edgewise.

Despite this, Lady Catherine directed most of her inquiries toward me with only a few exceptions made for comments meant for Mr. Collins, who answered in his usual fawning manner.

"How is it that you came to know my nephew, Miss Bennet?" she asked suddenly, fixing me with a sharp gaze.

I met her pointed question with a calm smile that hid my true panic. *Here it was. Here was the lie.* "As I mentioned before, your Ladyship, we met at a ball in London. Lady Bearing's ball to be precise."

"Yes, I do recall," Lady Catherine said. "But you must tell me again. How is it that you came to be engaged so quickly? Fitzwilliam has never been one for hasty decisions."

The gentleman across from me seemed to hold his breath.

"As I have said, it was... unexpected," I said carefully. "But we both knew that our feelings for each other were true and strong."

Her ladyship snorted. "Feelings? What do *feelings* have to do with anything? This is about securing a future for our family and our name."

"Indeed," Mr. Darcy said, speaking up for the first time since dinner had begun. "But surely compatibility and affection are important factors to consider when entering into a marriage."

Lady Catherine glared at him. "That may be so, Fitzwilliam, but it is not the *sole* reason for marriage. And besides, how do we know that Miss Bennet is compatible with our family?"

"I assure you, your Ladyship," I said calmly. "I will do everything in my power to prove myself worthy of your family's name and honor."

Lady Catherine sniffed, but did not reply. Instead, she turned her attention back to Mr. Collins, who began to eagerly recount the tale of his most recent interactions with his parishioners.

Mr. Darcy's frown was difficult to read, but I felt certain that he was worried that our ruse would be discovered.

For now, we had made it through dinner without incident.

As the meal came to a close, Lady Catherine announced that she would retire to her private parlor and invited us all to join her for tea.

Charlotte and I rose from our seats and followed Lady Catherine out of the dining room. Mr. Collins fell into step behind us and I kept my shoulders straight as we walked down the corridor toward her Ladyship's private parlor.

Her ladyship was seated in a plush velvet chair near the fire as a silent uniformed maid poured tea and distributed it amongst us. The moment Lady Catherine de Bourgh turned her scrutinizing gaze upon me, I knew that the test had begun. Her icy blue eyes seemed to bore into my very soul, seeking out any weakness or flaw that might render me unworthy of Mr. Darcy's hand.

"Tell me, Miss Bennet," she began, her voice dripping with condescension, "what is your opinion on the accomplishments a young lady of good breeding should possess?"

I took a deep breath before responding, Mr. Collins had warned me that Lady Catherine was quite concerned about such things. "A lady of good breeding, ma'am, should be well-versed in the art of conversation, have a thorough knowledge of music, singing, drawing, dancing, and the modern languages. Though I do have an opinion on the ancient ones as well. She should also possess a certain... grace in her air and manner of walking, and the tone of her voice."

"Indeed," Lady Catherine replied, her eyes narrowing ever so slightly as she assessed my answer. "And do you consider yourself accomplished in these areas, Miss Bennet?"

"By no means as much as I ought to be," I admitted, feeling the weight of her scrutiny bearing down upon me. "But I am confident in my own abilities and strive to improve myself in every way possible."

"Confidence is all well and good, but misplaced confidence can be a dangerous thing," she warned, her gaze never wavering from mine.

Throughout this exchange, I could not help but fidget nervously with the hem of my gown, keenly aware of Mr. Darcy's watchful eye and the potential consequences of my failure to impress his formidable aunt. To my relief, he kept his eyes carefully averted, focusing intently on the delicate patterns of the china before him.

As my tea cooled in my cup, Lady Catherine continued her merciless interrogation. She inquired about my family, our connections, and the extent of our fortune—or lack thereof. Though I endeavored to answer each question with grace and candor, I could not help but feel the strain of maintaining our ruse. My heart pounded in my chest, and I was certain that my irritation would begin to show at any moment.

"Your mother's family is from trade, is it not?" Lady Catherine asked, her tone sharp, as if the mere mention of such a connection was distasteful.

"Indeed, ma'am," I replied, struggling to keep my voice steady. "My grandfather was a successful merchant, and we are proud of our heritage. My uncle has a successful warehouse in London."

"Ah, I see." Her eyes flickered to Mr. Darcy for a brief moment before returning to me. "Well, one must make do with the connections one has, I suppose."

I clenched my hands beneath the table, willing myself to remain composed in the face of her thinly veiled disdain. The air between us crackled with tension, and I feared that at any moment, it would all come crashing down around us.

When I thought I would not be able to bear her ladyship's

questions any longer, she set down her teacup upon the table near her elbow and cleared her throat.

"I believe it is time for us to say goodnight to you, Mr. Collins," Mr. Darcy said briskly. "It has been a most... diverting evening. Mrs. Collins, a pleasure to meet you."

I had a feeling that this action was something her nephew had recognized as a mark of Lady Catherine's waning interest in the conversation and company and I was grateful to him for his observation.

"Of course," Mr. Collins spluttered, seemingly embarrassed at not noticing the signs of his patroness' discomfort before Mr. Darcy. "A most wonderful evening, indeed."

"Miss Bennet, you may come to tea tomorrow," Lady Catherine said, ignoring the parson's fawning words. "I shall hear no arguments."

"Of course, your Ladyship," I replied. "I should be delighted."

"Indeed," Lady Catherine muttered. With a wave of her hand she dismissed us all. "Fitzwilliam will see you to the door," she said grumpily as she rose from her chair. "Rodgers— Fetch me a glass of brandy!"

After some hastily spoken good evenings, Mr. Darcy ushered us toward the foyer. Someone had called for the carriage beforehand, and it stood ready in the courtyard to carry us back to the parsonage. For myself, I would have preferred the walk so that I could mutter my frustrations into the dark.

"Her Ladyship's third best carriage," Mr. Collins said with some awe as he held out his hand to assist Charlotte as she climbed into the vehicle.

"Indeed," Mr. Darcy said briskly.

"Miss Bennet," he said. "Might I speak with you a moment."

"Of course, Mr. Darcy," I replied with a sweetness that was almost mockery. "We are engaged, after all."

Mr. Collins jumped up into the carriage, but I could feel the parson's eyes upon us as I turned to face Mr. Darcy.

"You did very well," he said in a hushed tone.

"I know it," I replied.

"I must speak with you tomorrow."

"Fortunately for you, I have been commanded to come to tea," I said. "You may speak with me then."

"No— Miss Bennet—"

"Good evening, Mr. Darcy," I said as I laid her hand upon his elbow and smiled at him. This politeness was growing tedious, and I wanted nothing more than to be alone. "We shall speak again very soon."

My words were for no one's benefit than Mr. Collins and Charlotte, and I knew that they were listening intently for any nuance or falsehood that could be questioned.

"Indeed," he said. "Never soon enough."

I turned away and he followed me to the carriage to offer his assistance, but I very purposefully ignored his hand and stepped up into the carriage without difficulty.

Stubborn man.

I did not look at him as the driver snapped his whip over the horses' backs and the carriage lurched into motion.

"What a wonderful evening," Mr. Collins said brightly. "Do you not agree, cousin?"

"Indeed," I murmured, but Mr. Collins was not listening to me as he launched into a grandly one-sided discussion of the grandeur of the Darcy and de Bourgh families and how truly fortunate I was to be joining such an illustrious family.

I looked out the window at the darkness and the cloudless sky splashed with stars and wished that I could have been home in Hertfordshire.

I should never have come to Hunsford.

seven

"COUSIN, YOU MUST LISTEN TO ME," Mr. Collins begged. "Being invited to Lady Catherine de Bourgh's private parlor for tea is a very important step— You must be prepared—"

"I believe that I am quite well enough prepared, Mr. Collins," I replied shortly. "Lady Catherine can do nothing about my engagement to her nephew."

"Be that as it may," the parson said nervously. "You would do well to secure her ladyship's favor. There are not many who can count Lady Catherine de Bourgh among their friends—"

"I imagine not," I muttered.

Charlotte hid her smile behind her teacup as her husband spluttered his indignation at my words.

"Cousin Elizabeth, you are being most unreasonable," Mr. Collins choked out.

"I do not believe so," I said. "Lady Catherine is determined to know me better, and I will not disguise who I am, or anything about my family that she might wish to know. Mr. Darcy has already deemed me worthy of his esteem—"

It was difficult to protest such things. The engagement was

false. My feelings for him, and my devotion to this ruse, were false... And my anger toward him remained. If I was to be forced to maintain this farce for much longer, I would be hard-pressed to keep a civil tongue.

But there was no way out of this.

None that I could see.

"Mr. Collins, I simply wish to enjoy my tea in peace," I said. "Charlotte— if you will forgive me, I need some fresh air. Shall I put on another kettle for tea?"

Charlotte nodded, half-rising from her chair. "Shall I assist you?"

"No, I beg you. I simply need to... clear my head."

"Do hurry back, cousin," Mr. Collins begged. "There is much for us to discuss when it comes to Lady Catherine's likes and dislikes—there are several topics of conversation that must be avoided at all costs!"

I walked down the corridor, seething with anger, my mind consumed with thoughts of Mr. Darcy and his stubbornness. How could he expect me to play along with this charade when all I wanted was to be away from him?

I wished that I had never met him.

It was infuriating that I had to sit through these polite gatherings while pretending to be engaged to a man who I could barely stand to be in the same room with.

I walked into the kitchen and set a kettle over the fire to boil. I crossed my arms over my chest and stared into the fire. But I could not simply stand there and watch the kettle—it was too stuffy, and I was far too angry.

I pushed open the kitchen door and stepped out into the gardens. A cool breeze washed over me, bringing with it the sweet fragrance of blooming flowers and the tang of the herbs that grew nearby. It was a welcome relief from the stuffy confines of the kitchen.

How much longer could I stay at the parsonage? How much longer would I be expected to keep up this charade? This... mockery of an engagement?

Motion at the garden gate caught my eye, and I looked up in surprise at Mr. Darcy who stood there, frozen in place.

"Mr. Darcy," I said warily. "What brings you here so early?"

"Are you— Are you all right?" he choked out.

"I am not," I snapped. "Mr. Collins seems to think that I need very careful preparation as to how to speak and behave in the presence of Lady Catherine de Bourgh. You would think that I had been commanded to appear before the Queen!"

Mr. Darcy started to chuckle, and then cleared his throat.

Was he mocking me?

"I am sorry," I said.

"Did you come to speak with Mr. Collins?" I demanded, hoping that would be his reason for being here at such an early hour.

"Indeed, not," he said. "I need to speak with you. It is important."

I nodded slowly and walked toward the garden gate. "I cannot be in that house a moment longer," I muttered as he opened the gate and stepped aside to allow me to pass.

We walked together down the path until we reached a fenced paddock. A number of fine horses grazed in the wild-flower dappled fields and I tried my best to take a deep breath and calm the angry beat of my heart.

I braced my arms against the fence and leaned against it. We stood in silence for a few moments, the only sound being the rustling of leaves in the breeze.

"Well? Something important?" I said.

"I have found a way to end this false engagement," Mr. Darcy said after a moment.

I could not help my skepticism. "What is it?" I asked cautiously.

"I must speak to your father," he replied. "Immediately."

I could feel the twist in my expression as confusion and anger coursed through me. "What are you talking about? Why would you want to do that?"

"I have not earned his permission to court you," he said calmly. "Therefore, he may refuse my request. It shall be official, and there will be no shame for you, or your family."

"No shame upon my family for *your* lie," I spat out.

"No one was supposed to know," he protested. "But that has become unavoidable. This is the only way to set things right... and quickly. If we continue with this deception, it will only end in disaster for both of us."

"And what about your aunt?" I said pointedly. "She will not take kindly to this turn of events."

"She will not," he agreed, "but I shall speak to her. I will explain the situation and take full responsibility for my actions."

I searched his face for any sign of deception or mockery, but I found none. "I hope you understand the gravity of what you have done, Mr. Darcy."

"I do," he said sincerely. "I promised you that I would make this right. And I intend to do precisely that."

I nodded slowly and looked away. I could not deny that I was relieved to hear his solution, but I did not like the fact that this deception would have to be brought to my very doorstep. "Very well, then. I shall write to my father and tell him that you will visit. But I will leave the explanations for *you* to make."

"Thank you."

"But let me be clear," I added firmly. "This does not mean that I can simply forget everything that has happened between us. Or that I will forgive you."

"I understand," he said quietly.

"Very well." I straightened up and took a deep breath. "Now, if you will excuse me, Mr. Darcy, I must return to Rosings Park for tea with Lady Catherine."

"Be careful," he warned. "She will not be kind, though she believes herself to be."

"I had assumed as much," I said. "Somehow the ladies of this level of society all behave the same... I am grateful that I am not in their presence very often."

"And why might that be?"

I smiled briefly. "They do not take kindly to my lack of accomplishment in the areas they understand... A young lady who does not draw or paint or play pianoforte. I do not sing... There is nothing I do that is pleasing or acceptable to them."

"Do your accomplishments please *you*?" he asked after a moment.

This time, my smile was genuine. "They do," I said. "Very much. My books and maps do not judge my singing or how quickly I can transcribe a concerto."

"Indeed, not," he replied.

I turned and walked away, my skirts rustling in the breeze. This was, indeed, a good solution. My father would not hesitate to set things right and free me from this falsehood. This... situation that had been forced upon me. He would come to my rescue because I could not save myself.

* * *

UPON THE APPOINTED HOUR, clad in a modest yet fashionable gown, and armed with a reluctant knowledge of Lady Catherine's many dislikes and a smaller list of subjects that she approved of, I entered Rosings Park with a heart full of dread.

The grand manor loomed before me, its opulence both threatening and awe-inspiring. I had no doubt that was the entire purpose of its design.

I was suddenly glad that Lord de Bourgh was not long deceased. I did not think that he would be any more agreeable than his formidable wife.

The butler led me down the corridor without saying more than a few words to me. It was odd to be judged by a servant who seemed to consider himself above me. But I supposed such a thing was possible when in service to a family like the de Bourgh's.

The butler paused in front of a door and after looking me up and down, he opened it and entered ahead of me. Already on edge, I took a breath and followed him into the room. I was immediately struck by the opulence that surrounded me. Every surface gleamed with an air of wealth and privilege, from the gilded mirrors to the plush velvet settees.

Lady Catherine was seated in a large velvet upholstered chair with her feet resting upon a matching settle, her imperious gaze fixed upon me as I crossed the threshold.

"Ah, Miss Bennet, punctuality is a quality that every young lady should aspire to," she drawled, her voice dripping with condescension. "Do come in and take a seat."

"Thank you, Lady Catherine," I replied, maintaining my composure as I settled into the proffered chair. A uniformed footman appeared at my elbow, bearing a tray laden with fine china and assorted delicacies. As he poured the tea, I could feel Lady Catherine's eyes boring into me, assessing my every movement.

"Your dress is quite... quaint," she remarked, her lips curling into a disdainful smile. "A charming reflection of your... limited upbringing, no doubt."

Her Ladyship's attitude was not much different from the

evening before. I suspected that she liked to know the... order of things. She liked to be certain that everyone knew their place.

"Indeed, Lady Catherine," I replied evenly, refusing to rise to her bait. "My family has always valued simplicity and practicality."

"Of course," she sniffed, waving a dismissive hand. "With five daughters to feed and clothe, it is not a surprise that such virtues have been imparted to you."

I bristled at her words, but held my tongue as I sipped my tea in silence. My thoughts swirled like leaves caught in a tempest, a mixture of indignation and disbelief at her blatant snobbery. Yet there was something in her haughty demeanor that spoke to a deeply ingrained belief in her own superiority—one that would not be easily swayed.

"Miss Bennet," Lady Catherine continued, her tone heavy with scorn, "I must confess, I find your presence here at Rosings Park most... curious. It is not often that a young lady of your... station is granted such an opportunity."

"Opportunity, Lady Catherine?" I asked, my voice strained with the effort of remaining civil.

"Indeed," she replied, her eyes narrowing like a predator circling its prey. "Your recent engagement to my nephew. I find it most perplexing that you would presume to elevate yourself to such heights. Tell me, how did you come to obtain an invitation to Lady Bearing's ball?"

"Your ladyship," I said, struggling to contain my ire, "I assure you, I have not presumed anything." My hands clenched unconsciously around the delicate teacup, the porcelain creaking ominously beneath my fingers. "And my invitation was obtained by my aunt, Mrs. Gardiner. She is friends with Lady Bearing. Her ladyship also was kind enough to allow me to borrow one of her daughter's gowns for the occasion."

"How kind of her," Lady Catherine sneered. "I did not

presume that you would have dared to attend such a function in... muslin."

"I would not presume—"

"I somehow knew that this would be a problem," she sighed. "And so I have taken the liberty of making some arrangements for the wedding."

"You— you have?" I choked out.

"Indeed," her ladyship snapped. "The guest list must be made up of the most important and influential members of our society. Your friends and relations will not be welcome, so it is not necessary to inform them of such things. The wedding will be held here at Rosings Park. Mr. Collins shall preside over the ceremony— I did hope that the future Mrs. Darcy would wear lace for her wedding, but I do not think the expense should be spared in this case."

I seethed with anger. I did not want this wedding—this wedding would not be taking place. But if it were, this was what she had planned?

"I would not presume—" I murmured.

"Ah," she sneered, "but perhaps that is precisely the problem, Miss Bennet. A woman of your background could never *presume* to understand the responsibilities and obligations that accompany a union with one such as Mr. Darcy. I must say that I am quite surprised at his lack of judgment in this regard. Why, your very presence here at Rosings Park is an affront to propriety and decorum."

"Enough!" I cried, my anger finally boiling over. The teacup shattered in my grasp, shards of porcelain scattering across the polished floor. I rose from my seat, my face flushed with fury and humiliation. "Lady Catherine, I will not be spoken to in such a manner!"

"Miss Bennet," she hissed, her eyes blazing with contempt, "you forget yourself."

"Indeed, I do not," I retorted, my voice shaking with emotion as I rose from my seat. "And I shall take my leave of Rosings Park forthwith."

With those parting words, I strode across the room and wrenched the door open.

"Come back here," Lady Catherine cried, but I did not turn and quickened my pace, almost running into the corridor.

"I say, come back here at once!" Lady Catherine cried again.

"I shall not," I called over my shoulder, and then I realized that I was not alone in the corridor. Mr. Darcy stood there, inches away from me. I had almost charged straight into him. "Mr. Darcy," I said, my cheeks burning with anger. "Did you come to spy on me?"

"No— Indeed I did not—"

"Miss Bennet!"

With a grunt of anger, I pushed the parlor door closed to muffle Lady Catherine's indignant voice. I brushed a stray curl off my forehead and met the gentleman's incredulous gaze.

"Your aunt—"

Mr. Darcy winced and gestured toward the foyer. I nodded and fell into step beside him. "Is my aunt planning the wedding already?"

"Not only that, she has already made the guest list, and chosen the fabric for my wedding gown."

"Ah—"

"Ah?" I snapped. "That is all you can say? She has also made it clear that my *family* need not be invited. Only *important* guests."

The gentleman grimaced, but I had a feeling he had been expecting all of this.

He held up his hands. "I have made the arrangements as you requested. I shall be leaving for Hertfordshire in a few hours' time."

"Good," I snapped. "I shall be doing the same very shortly. I have had my fill of Hunsford and Rosings Park. By the time I arrive at Longbourn I shall expect that everything will be done."

"You may have my word upon it," he said.

"I do not trust your word," I said vehemently.

"And you have every right to feel that way," he said with some chagrin, "which is why I am leaving sooner than later."

"I hope I do not see you in Meryton," I said stiffly. "But I wish you a safe journey. The roads are not the best in the country."

"Indeed, I thank you," he said. "I hope that your remaining days here are pleasant ones."

"They will be if I do not step foot in this house again," I muttered.

"You can be certain of that," he chuckled. "My aunt does not take kindly to anyone walking out of her presence without being dismissed."

I glanced over my shoulder at the empty corridor behind us. "Then we should hurry, I will not allow that horrid butler to drag me back into that room."

"Indeed."

We walked quickly, each of us glancing back over our shoulders to be certain that we were not being followed. I thought I heard Lady Catherine's voice echo in the corridor, but Rosings' butler did not appear to escort me back to the parlor, and we reached the foyer without seeing anyone who might have stopped us or enquired as to our business.

As we reached the foyer, Mr. Darcy pulled the door open and stood aside to allow me to exit the house. "Good day, Mr. Darcy," I said quickly, relieved to have escaped mostly unscathed. "Let us hope that we do not meet again."

"Good day, Miss Bennet," he said, though I noticed a flash of something that seemed like disappointment on his handsome face.

Could he really feel some regret that this lie would be coming to an end?

I smiled before I could stop myself. He had made this an almost painless process—despite the lie, I found that I could not deny that I had enjoyed his company.

Impossible.

I turned away and waited for the sound of the door closing before I could finally take a full breath.

Charlotte would be upset to hear that I wished to leave, but I had no doubt that Mr. Collins would be very pleased to be rid of me, especially when he was informed of my terrible behavior in Lady Catherine's presence.

I smiled at the memory of the older woman's indignant and shocked expression when I had broken the teacup.

My laughter echoed over the grassy field and I turned my face toward the sunshine. The sooner I could leave this place the better. I had a life to live... and if Mr. Darcy kept his word, I would be free to do so.

But then I remembered the look in his eyes when we had parted.

What if he had no intention of breaking our engagement?

What then?

eight

I HAD INTENDED to spend a few more days at Hunsford to give Mr. Darcy time to perform his obligation—but as soon as Mr. Collins discovered how my teatime at Rosings Park had progressed, I was very hastily bundled into a carriage and sent on my way back to Hertfordshire.

I did not even have time to send word to my aunt and could not stop in London to stay with them—my hope of avoiding Mr. Darcy's visit to Longbourn dwindled all the more.

I had not yet told Jane of what had happened, and I had intended not to, but it seemed that I would have to do precisely that.

As the carriage rolled along the bumpy roads, I couldn't help but feel a sense of unease.

My thoughts kept returning to Mr. Darcy and our fabricated engagement. What if he refused to break it off and revealed the truth to everyone?

What if my family found out about this elaborate lie? And that I had been a part of it in the end.

I felt a lump form in my throat as I thought about the shame that would bring upon my family.

I mulled over how best to broach the subject with Jane. She was always so kind-hearted; I did not relish the thought of bringing her disappointment and heartache.

Finally, as the carriage pulled into the courtyard, I knew there was no avoiding it. I took a deep breath and braced myself for the conversation that awaited me.

My sisters raced out of the house to welcome me home, and I embraced each of them in turn and accepted their kisses as they all tried to speak at once about what I had missed while I had been away in London.

Jane, as usual, waited for the other girls to all have their turn before they ran back into the house calling for our mother. Mama was most likely in the parlor, I could see the twitch of the curtains as she rushed back to her chair to pretend that she did not know I had arrived.

It was an old game, but one that she never tired of.

"Jane," I said as we walked toward the house. "I must tell you something."

She looked at me expectantly. "Of course, Lizzy. What is it?"

"Do you recall that I wrote to you about attending Lady Bearing's ball while I was in London?"

"I do," she replied. "Everyone was very envious of your good fortune."

I let out a heavy sigh. "They should not be. I should not have gone to that ball."

"But did you not meet a charming gentleman there?" Jane asked in surprise. "I do not recall his name—"

"Mr. Darcy," I said.

"Yes!" Jane breathed. "That was his name. But why—"

"Oh, Jane," I said. "When I went to visit dear Charlotte—"

"Charlotte! But how is she now that she is Mrs. Collins?"

"She is very well, Jane— Well, she is not very well at all... but that is not the point—"

"Girls! Come inside," my mother shouted from the doorway. "It is cold, and you will catch your death if you tarry too long!"

It was not cold, and we would catch nothing, but our mother was very clearly in a mood... and there would be no escaping it.

"You must tell me everything tonight," Jane said as we quickened our pace to return to the house before our mother lost her temper entirely.

"I promise," I said.

I was frustrated, but what I had to tell her would have to wait until after supper.

During supper, my mother chattered away about the latest gossip from Meryton, and my father dutifully listened while adding a comment here and there. My younger sisters were engaged in their private conversations, while Jane looked at me expectantly, waiting for supper to be over so that I could tell her what was bothering me.

She was a patient soul, but by the time we were able to go up to bed she was barely able to wait until the door of our chamber closed before she demanded that I tell her the truth.

"Lizzy— I have been trying to guess at what you were going to tell me but I confess that I have driven myself half mad with it!"

I sat down on my bed and began to unpin my hair. "Jane, it is... difficult to describe."

"You met the gentleman in London?"

"Yes.

"And then?"

"And then I saw him again while I was at Hunsford!"

"At Hunsford! But why would he be there?"

"He was visiting his aunt," I said. "Lady Catherine de Bourgh of Rosings Park."

Jane frowned. "Mr. Collins' patroness?"

"The very same."

"Oh, dear."

"Indeed, but that is not the worst of it," I said. "Mr. Darcy... he... He told Lady Catherine that we were engaged to be married."

Jane gasped aloud and sank down on the bed beside me.

"Lizzy— Are you truly engaged?"

"I most certainly am not," I said indignantly. "The gentleman lied. He commissioned a portrait of me—"

"A portrait!"

I leaned forward to open my valise and pulled out the velvet wrapped miniature. Jane snatched it out of my hands and unwrapped it quickly.

"Oh, Lizzy," she breathed. "It is... a perfect likeness!"

"I know," I said grimly.

The portrait had, indeed, been captured with such care and attention to detail that it seemed almost lifelike.

"Lizzy— what if this Mr. Darcy does, indeed, have some affection for you?"

"For me?" I scoffed, incredulous at the suggestion. But the seed of doubt had been planted, and I found myself unable to dismiss it entirely.

Jane looked down at the portrait again and shook her head. "Such a fine likeness could only have been made by someone who truly admired you," Jane said softly, as if the very words might shatter my fragile composure.

"Admired me..." I repeated, tasting the unfamiliar idea. My heart raced, torn between the indignation I had felt at Mr. Darcy's deception and the new possibility that Jane had presented. "But that is impossible. He did not even know me when he had that painted. But that does not excuse what happened. He used my portrait, and my name, to pretend to an engagement that did not exist!"

"But, how did you discover it?"

"He told me," I said miserably. "Lady Catherine had demanded to meet me, and I just so happened to be at Hunsford."

"Quite the coincidence," Jane breathed.

"Indeed. A terrible coincidence."

We sat in silence for several minutes, both lost in our thoughts. My mind was racing with conflicting emotions. I couldn't deny the fact that part of me was flattered by the idea that Mr. Darcy may have had some affection for me, but at the same time, I was hurt and angered by his deception.

"Lizzy, what are you going to do?" Jane asked softly, breaking the silence.

"Mr. Darcy is coming to Longbourn to speak to Papa. I had hoped that he would have come and gone before I returned home... but it seems that he was delayed in his journey."

"Speak to Papa," Jane said, "whatever for?"

"He does not have Papa's permission to court me," I said. "Papa must tell him that the engagement is broken and that he is never to see me again."

"Have you spoken to Papa?"

"No," I said. "And I do not intend to. I do not wish to make Mr. Darcy's admission of guilt any easier. He must explain it to Papa and beg for his refusal. I did not give my consent for this... impossible engagement, and I will not assist him any further. He will tell Papa the truth, he promised to do, and he will face the consequences. And Papa's ire."

"A wise decision," Jane said. "I do not know what I would do—"

"I did not think I would ever be in such a situation," I sighed. I fell back on the bed, grabbed my pillow and placed it over my face so that I could groan aloud.

"Lizzy," Jane laughed as she pulled the pillow off my face.

"You are being far too dramatic. It must not have been too terrible a thing to pretend to be engaged to a handsome gentleman with a good fortune."

I grabbed for my pillow but Jane held it out of my reach.

"Jane! I did not— I did not think of it like that. I was too... angry with him."

"A pity," Jane said. "Then it is fortunate that it will be over before anyone finds out."

I nodded. "That is my hope."

"If Mama were to find out, the news would reach Lady Lucas immediately..."

"That was what I was afraid of," I said with a grimace. "I can only hope that Charlotte has not already written to her mother about it."

"Let us hope not."

As we began to get ready for bed, I couldn't shake the feeling of uncertainty that weighed heavily on my heart. Despite my anger towards Mr. Darcy's deceit, I couldn't deny the fact that I had been captivated by him since we had first met at Lady Bearing's ball.

As I lay in bed and closed my eyes, images of Mr. Darcy danced through my mind, causing my heart to flutter. But as quickly as those thoughts came, they were replaced by memories of how I had felt when his deception had first been revealed.

I knew that I needed time to sort through my feelings and come to a decision about what to do next. But for now, all I could do was try to get some rest and hope that the morning would bring some clarity.

* * *

JANE and I were seated in the parlor with our mending in our laps. I was, for once, grateful for the normalcy of the situation. Kitty and Lydia argued over what they would wear to the upcoming regimental ball, but I was not paying attention to him. I was more worried about when Mr. Darcy would arrive. I did not wish to see him, or speak to him... and I did not want to be in the house when he came—but how was I to know?

"Do you know when?" Jane asked as though she could hear my thoughts.

"No," I replied softly. "But I hope that he does not wait too long... every hour that passes is making me more anxious—"

As if summoned by our conversation, the sound of hooves on gravel drew our attention to the window. My heart leapt into my throat as I recognized the tall, dark figure approaching Longbourn.

"Jane, it is Mr. Darcy!" I gasped, feeling both dread and anticipation surge within me.

Mr. Darcy dismounted his horse with practiced grace, his expression serious and determined.

Lydia and Kitty rushed to the window.

"A gentleman," Kitty squealed. "I shall go and meet him!"

"You shall not!" Lydia cried. They pushed and pulled at each other in an effort to leave the parlor first.

"Jane— I cannot be here," I choked out.

"Go upstairs," Jane whispered urgently. "Run! Lydia and Kitty will delay him long enough."

I nodded and ran from the room as my mother called after me. Jane nodded reassuringly as she stood at the door of the parlor and I raced up the stairs toward our bedchamber. I stopped at the top of the stairs and crouched by the railing. I knew that I should go into our room, but I could not deny that I wished to see him—only for a moment. To hear his voice...

Just once more.

"Who are you?" Lydia demanded, her strident voice echoing up the stairs. My cheeks burned with embarrassment to know that she was the first introduction the gentleman would have to my family.

"I am Mr. Darcy," he replied.

"Are you here to see Papa?" Lydia demanded.

"Lydia!" Jane cried from the parlor. Lydia laughed wildly and slammed the door shut before she ran away screeching with laughter at her own rude boldness.

I waited, holding my breath, and then heard the door open again.

"I do apologize," Jane's voice echoed up the stairs and I let out the breath I had been holding. Jane would make everything right. "My sister— she should not have—"

"It is quite all right," the gentleman said.

"What was your name?" Jane asked.

"Mr. Darcy, Fitzwilliam Darcy."

"You are most welcome to Longbourn," Jane said, and I could hear the smile in her voice. "Please, do come in."

"I have come to see Mr. Arthur Bennet," the gentleman said as he stepped over the threshold.

"Of course," Jane said. "We did not know when you might arrive, but Papa is expecting you."

"And you are?"

"Jane," she replied simply. "Elizabeth is my sister. Lydia is the one who greeted you, and Kitty is too shy to come out of the parlor."

There was another shriek of laughter from the two youngest girls and I rolled my eyes heavenward with embarrassment.

"Mary is in the parlor," Jane continued, "but she will not come out. Mama is in town visiting with Lady Lucas."

"I see," he said. "And your father?"

"In his study, as always," Jane replied. "This way, if you please."

I listened to their footsteps as Jane led him down the corridor toward my father's study and then crept down the stairs, being careful to avoid the creaky third step so that I would not be caught spying.

The gentleman knocked on the door, the sound echoing in the house.

"Enter."

The door creaked and I peered around the railing to catch sight of the gentleman as he entered my father's study, but I only saw the door close behind him.

"Lizzy," Jane hissed, her voice making me jump in surprise.

"Jane, you frightened me."

Jane smiled and laughed gently. "I do apologize, but I did not think you would be so eager to see someone you seem to dislike so much."

"I am not eager," I retorted.

"Oh, indeed," Jane mocked me. "Will you listen at the door?"

"I—"

Jane smiled. "You do not need to be embarrassed, my dear. I would wish to do the same."

"To be sure that he does as he promised," I said. "Nothing more."

"Nothing more," Jane echoed.

I could hardly allow such a momentous conversation to take place without our observation.

I crept down the hallway with Jane following behind me.

I could hear voices from behind the door, but they were muffled. I laid my ear against the cool wood and closed my eyes, but the voices were still indistinct.

The hallway seemed to grow smaller as the tense moments

passed, our breaths held in anticipation. I could feel the hot pressure of Jane's hand gripping my arm, her own anxiety a mirror of mine.

My heart pounded fiercely against my ribcage, each beat echoing the war within me—a battle between anger, confusion, and hurt, tempered by a growing sense of attraction towards Mr. Darcy.

"Lizzy, what are you doing?"

Kitty and Lydia had discovered us but Jane hushed them quickly lest we be discovered.

Finally, I could hear my father's voice.

"I see," he said shortly. "And why have you come here?"

"I have come to ask you to reject my proposal," Mr. Darcy replied. "Our engagement was false, of course, but with the swiftness of it, there would have been no time to ask your permission for this union. All that need be done is for you to reject my suit. Elizabeth would be free of this falsehood, and I can return to my own life."

Silence fell over the room and I wondered what was happening.

"And what is it about you that I would reject?" my father asked. "What is your income?"

His question sent a cold chill down my spine.

"I— Ten thousand a year, I should think," Mr. Darcy replied.

"And you have an estate?"

"I do. Pemberley, in Derbyshire."

My father paused. "And do you enjoy hunting?"

"No, Sir," mr. Darcy replied quickly. "I am a steward of my estate and do not delight in killing the creatures that live upon it."

"I see," my father said. "This portrait that you commissioned— It was a good likeness?"

"Indeed," the gentleman said, and his tone was one of

surprise. "The artist was very talented and I paid him well for his time."

"And your description of the subject must have been very fine, indeed, to produce such an excellent result that Lady Catherine de Bourgh was not disappointed in seeing Elizabeth in the flesh."

"I—"

"Papa," I whispered. "What are you doing?"

"If you will dismiss me, Sir," Mr. Darcy continued, "I will return to my lodgings at the White Horse Inn. From there I shall return to Rosings Park to tell my aunt of the end of my engagement and from there I shall go back to Pemberley..."

My father cleared his throat loudly and there was silence in the room. "No," he said.

"I beg your pardon?" Mr. Darcy's question echoed my own shock.

"You shall not be dismissed," my father said. "I do not reject your proposal, Mr. Darcy," he continued. "In fact, I endorse it wholeheartedly."

No... that was not what I wanted—

Papa!

I let out a choked noise and there was a sudden silence in the room. Jane pulled me away from the door.

"Mama is coming," she hissed. "Hurry!"

As Jane pulled me back to the parlor, my thoughts swirled like autumn leaves caught in a whirlwind. What would become of us now?

The Lucas' carriage pulled into the courtyard and my mother alighted with a wide smile upon her face.

"Girls," she called out. "You will never believe what has happened— Netherfield Park has been let at last! I have it on good authority that the gentleman is of a very fine character, indeed!"

I swallowed hard as my mother swept into the house and ushered us toward the parlor. "I have a good deal of gossip to tell you," she exclaimed.

The sound of the study door as it creaked open filled me with dread.

No.

"Mrs. Bennet—" my father called out. "You have returned at the most opportune moment. I have something of great import to tell you!"

Panic tightened its grip on my throat.

This should have been an easy meeting—Mr. Darcy should have made his apology and my father would have accepted it on my behalf and then I would be released from the gentleman's haste deception.

But he had done precisely the opposite.

"What is it, Mr. Bennet, I am *very* busy," my mother replied in a shrill voice. "Did you know that your daughters will need new gowns for the regimental ball?"

"I am only concerned about one daughter needing a new gown," my father said. My mother's eyes widened as she caught sight of the gentleman who strode out of my father's study.

"Who is this? You are most welcome to Longbourn, sir," she said with a charming smile. "My daughter Jane did not tell me that anyone was here—Mr. Bennet—"

"This is Mr. Fitzwilliam Darcy," my father replied. "He has come here to ask for my permission to marry our Lizzy."

My mother's eyes widened and her hand flew to her hair as her mouth dropped open. "Lizzy— But, Mr. Bennet—"

"I know, it is a shock, indeed. Lizzy has spoken of no one—"

"Lizzy and her secrets," my mother fumed. "But Mr. Darcy you must come and have tea—"

"No, no, wife. You will not overwhelm the gentleman," my father chuckled, "he has rooms at the inn in Meryton, and that is where he must go. But he shall return tomorrow evening for supper, will you not, Mr. Darcy?"

"I—"

"Good man," Mr. Bennet said with a quick smile. He clapped the gentleman on the shoulder once more and turned him toward the door. "You are most welcome here, Sir," he said. "Lizzy will be pleased to see that you have come."

"I—"

"Good day to you, Mr. Darcy," he said loudly. "We shall see you upon the morrow."

"Good day—"

Lydia and Kitty burst out laughing once more, and I pressed my back against the wall of the parlor so that I would not be seen as the gentleman passed by.

Jane stood in the doorway of the parlor to block his view of the room.

"You have made us all so happy," Jane said sweetly. "Lizzy will be overjoyed to hear that Papa has given his blessing."

I gritted my teeth and wished that I could scream.

"I look forward to hearing every detail of your meeting tomorrow evening over dinner," Jane said.

"Of course..."

A moment later the front door closed and my younger sisters shrieked with laughter as they ran into the parlor to embrace me and shout about what they would wear to the wedding.

Through the window, I watched Mr. Darcy as he untied his horse's reins from the fencepost, set his foot into the stirrup, and swung up into the saddle.

Through no fault of my own I seemed to find myself very much engaged...

Mr. Darcy's deception had become reality, and now there was no escape—for either of us.

nine

I HAD NOT WANTED THIS.

None of this.

My father had betrayed me, and he seemed so pleased with himself that I could not even look at him.

Even Jane who had promised to support me had shown that her loyalty lay with the very gentleman who had begun this very deception and set out to ruin my life without thinking of how it would affect me in the slightest.

And now he was coming to supper.

My mother was, of course, overjoyed with the news and demanded to know every detail of our courtship—a courtship that did not exist except in my imagination.

But I could not lie to my mother. Or any of them.

I managed, somehow, to delay all of their questions until supper the following evening, but fear and desperation gnawed at me for the remainder of the day, kept me wakeful all night, and the following morning I rose before the sun to pace the floor of the parlor to try and figure out what I could do to correct this terrible situation.

I waited for Mr. Hill to deliver tea to my father's parlor before I knocked on the door.

"Enter."

I pushed open the door and strode into the room, my cheeks hot as I prepared to confront my father.

"Papa— How could you," I blurted out.

His thick white eyebrows lifted slightly. "How could I?"

"How could you betray me so cruelly," I demanded. "How? Mr. Darcy came here to request your refusal of his proposal!"

"So he said," my father agreed. He laid his hands upon his ledger and laced his fingers together. "But Lizzy, what father could refuse so excellent a suitor for any of his daughters? If she ever found out what might have happened here, your mama would beat me over the head with her fan until I could not recall your names and she would still not be satisfied."

My mouth fell open. "Papa! This is my... happiness that you have traded away! Mr. Darcy *lied*. He used my likeness to *lie* about an engagement that never took place!"

"I understand your frustration, Lizzy," my father said with a heavy sigh. "But think of it this way. Mr. Darcy had the integrity to come here to break this engagement. He was true to his word. This engagement might not have begun as you might have wished, but you would be a fool to let this opportunity pass you by."

"But it's not real, Papa," I protested. "It's all a lie."

"The lie has become reality, Lizzy," my father said firmly. "I have made it so. And it would be a grave mistake to let it slip away."

I felt the anger inside of me beginning to boil over, but I bit my tongue and took a deep breath. "What do you suggest I do then?" I asked.

"Embrace it, my dear," my father replied with a shrug. "I have seen the portrait he commissioned. It is the truest likeness of you that I have ever seen. And if a gentleman who had only known you for a few hours could have described you so perfectly— I cannot believe that there is not something there that is worth discovering. And who knows? Perhaps you will find the happiness that you seek."

I stared at my father in disbelief. How could he be so cavalier about this situation? Did he not realize the gravity of what had happened?

"I—"

"There is nothing more to be said on the matter," he said firmly. "I have told your Mama, and by nightfall, all of Hertfordshire will know of your engagement."

"Papa—"

My father smiled at me and picked up his quill. "You will forgive me in time, child. But for now, I will accept your anger."

I let out a frustrated noise and wrenched open the door of his study.

"I will *never* forgive you."

"Good day, Lizzy," my father said without looking up from his ledger.

I slammed the door shut behind me and stormed through the house.

"Unforgivable," I muttered as I flung myself onto the couch. "Unforgivable."

* * *

I ENDURED a full day of my mother's questions and Kitty and Lydia's excited exclamations over how jealous they were, and questions about where we might live and where we might travel after we were married, and whether we would be married by the old parson who had presided over almost every birth, marriage, and death in Hertfordshire.

"I need to go for a walk," I exclaimed as I pushed myself out of my seat and lurched toward the parlor door.

I felt ill.

"Do not be long, Lizzy," my mother called after me. "Supper will be happening very soon, and we are expecting Mr. Darcy at any moment! You will want to be here when he arrives!"

I did not say anything as I pulled open the front door and stomped out of the house.

I walked across the courtyard and down the road. Perhaps I would be able to meet Mr. Darcy before he arrived. I needed to speak to him.

The sound of hoofbeats made me quicken my pace.

It was him. It had to be.

Anticipation, anger, and anxiety all warred within me for supremacy, but as the gentleman's silhouette came into view, anger won.

The gentleman pulled back on the reins and stood up in the stirrups as he caught sight of me.

"I say," he called out. "Is everything all right?"

"It certainly is not," I shouted back.

"Elizabeth?"

"Mr. Darcy!" I called out as he approached me. My skirts flared with the force of my pace and my cheeks burned with anger and the slight chill in the air. I realized at once that I was not wearing gloves or a bonnet, and I had left my shawl behind. But I did not care.

"You have betrayed me," I snarled.

"Elizabeth—"

"I listened at the door during your meeting with my father," I snapped. "You were supposed to come here and beg him to refuse you. To *refuse* this ridiculous arrangement—this *impossible* thing! But you have not!"

"Elizabeth, please—"

"Do not call me that," I snarled.

He swung down from his horse and approached me with his hands spread. "Miss Bennet— I *tried*."

"This is all your fault. All of it. You have stolen my future, Mr. Darcy and I shall not forgive you for it."

I glared at him, hands on my hips, and I relished the fact that it was obvious that he did not know what to say.

"And did you..." I demanded. "Did you ask for his permission? Or did he just... offer it?"

"I told him how this all came about," he said. "I told him everything, begged his forgiveness— And then I asked for him to refuse me. To make it known that he did not approve of me."

"But he did not."

"He— did not."

I narrowed my eyes at him, but before I could accuse him of anything more, he spoke again.

"I understand that this is not what you wanted," he said, his voice strained. "If you would like me to speak with your father and try to undo what has been done, then I will do so."

I hesitated for just a moment before I shook my head firmly. "No," I said. "As much as I would like to demand that you go immediately to demand him to change his mind, my mother has been informed of it. Which means that, even though I have just arrived home, that the entirety of Meryton will know about it before nightfall."

"I tried, truly—"

"It does not matter," I snapped. "My sisters believe that this is a fine joke and Lydia almost fell out of her chair laughing at my reaction to Mama's vehement congratulations and accusations of secret keeping."

"I—"

"Do not apologize again," I snapped. "You are expected at supper. And we shall be expected to tell the tale of our *great* romance and how you captured my heart and soul in a matter of days." Before I could stop myself, I stomped my foot and let out a furious noise. "We are *not* allies, Mr. Darcy," I warned him. "I will *never* forgive you for this. There will be no capitulation here. We shall speak more on this matter, but I have no intention of being a biddable bride. You did not *win* me, sir. You stole me."

"I— I understand," he said.

"Good. Come along then."

I turned away and stomped away down the road, back toward the house. Our relationship had begun as a fantasy, and now the lie would have to continue. At least for a little while.

As we walked towards Longbourn, I couldn't help but feel a knot form in my stomach. The tension between us was palpable, and I wondered how long we could keep up this act before we broke.

And which one of us would break first?

"Elizabeth," he said softly as we walked through the courtyard. "I understand how you must feel—"

"No, Mr. Darcy," I interrupted brusquely. "You do not understand. You have no idea of the repercussions of your actions."

"I realize that now," he replied solemnly. He laid a hand on my arm, and I resisted the urge to flinch away. I would not allow him that satisfaction. "But please believe me when I say that I will do everything in my power to make things right."

"And what would that be? Taking back your proposal?" I asked, my voice laced with bitterness. "You have already tried that and failed." I tugged my arm out of his grasp.

"I know that might not be possible," he admitted. "But I will do whatever it takes to make our agreement on paper reflect our true intentions."

I did not wait for him as he tied his horse's reins to the same fence post as he had the day before.

I could hear the crunch of his boots on the gravel as he followed me to the house. The evening would be horrible. I knew it already. I felt no better. All of his protestations and promises meant nothing.

My mother greeted the gentleman with open arms, exclaiming how happy she was that her daughter had finally caught herself a wealthy husband. The gentleman smiled politely, and ignored my pointed glare as my mother asked if he had any good friends who might be in need of a wife.

Ordinarily, I would have been embarrassed and scandalized by my mother's candor and brisk manners, but I had no wish to make the gentleman comfortable.

My father kissed my cheek even though I turned away, and greeted Mr. Darcy quietly and shook his hand warmly. But I could not deny him conversation for long... without my father, I would have no one to talk to apart from Jane.

Dinner was a blur of conversation and simple but hearty food that paled in comparison to the supper I had enjoyed at Rosings Park.

Even though I had eaten little of it, what I'd managed to eat had been exquisite.

I took every opportunity to glare at Mr. Darcy when I thought that no one was looking, and I hoped that he could feel my irritation all through the meal.

I barely spoke to him, instead choosing to engage in lively discussions with my sisters. I could feel him watching me, but I would not give him the satisfaction of glancing in his direction or favoring him with a smile even though he spoke very kindly to Mary and complimented her pianoforte playing.

After dinner, when the family retired to the parlor, my

mother insisted that Mr. Darcy should sit beside me upon the couch, but my father intervened.

"I believe Mr. Darcy would benefit from a little gentlemanly conversation and a glass of brandy," he said. "Will you join me in my study?"

"I will, indeed," Mr. Darcy said gratefully.

My mother made a small fuss about the gentleman's departure, but she could not deny Mr. Bennet's request.

I followed them, staying a few steps behind, but just outside the study door, I reached out and caught Mr. Darcy's elbow in a tight grip. He turned to look at me in surprise and I glared back at him.

"I hope you realize what you've done," she said coldly.

"I do," he replied softly. "And I hope you will forgive me."

"I do not want your apologies," I snapped. "They mean nothing."

"I know," he said and reached out to pry my hand off his arm and held it gently. "But please understand that I did everything in my power to reverse this situation."

I sighed heavily and leaned against the wall. "I know," I said after a moment. "And I appreciate that. But it doesn't change the fact that we're stuck in this... mess."

"What would you have me do?"

I snorted. "Go back in time and forget that you ever met me? No, no, that is impossible, is it not?" I shook my head. "We shall have to discuss what happens next. I have no plans to leave Hertfordshire, and I suspect that you would wish to return to your own estate?"

"I do."

"Then we shall have to compromise," I said stiffly as I pulled my hand from his gentle grasp. "A marriage will be taking place whether we wish for it or not. My mother has already begun her planning, and I daresay your aunt has already ordered the flowers from London."

The gentleman tried not to smile. "I would not doubt it."

"You will have to stay in Meryton for a time," I said. "There will be... expectations. And there is a regimental ball approaching. Mama will expect—"

"I have already extended my stay," I said.

I nodded, my lips pressed into a thin line.

"Elizabeth—"

I shook her head. "Good evening, Mr. Darcy," I said. "I shall speak to you soon, as it seems that I have no other choice. Do enjoy your brandy."

"I—"

Before he could say anything else, I turned and strode away from him toward the parlor and my sisters once more.

ten

THE REGIMENTAL BALL was the last event that I wished to attend... but I had no choice whatsoever. Mr. Darcy had given my father money for new gowns for all of us, and while I was overwhelmed by his generosity, I could not thank him for it.

I chose a gown that I wanted in a color that suited me well, but I did not wonder what he would think when he saw me, and I did not hope that he would be pleased by what I had purchased with his money.

Jane and the other girls had written to him to express their gratitude immediately, but I had said nothing.

I did not intend to say anything.

As with every ball, Jane styled my hair and pinned my dark curls into an elaborate pile on top of my head, and bound them with a dark blue velvet ribbon.

"Now, Lizzy," my mother said briskly as we climbed into the carriage. "Everyone expects that you will dance only with Mr. Darcy. That is permitted now."

I said nothing.

"But Jane, you shall dance with anyone you wish—although

Mr. Darcy did mention to your father that his friend Mr. Bingley is coming to the ball as well tonight. I expect that you will give him preference if he asks you for a dance."

"Of course, Mama," Jane replied softly.

My mother had, of course, already planned that Jane would be married before the new year. She had not yet determined how that would happen, but the goal was in place regardless.

As we entered the garrison ballroom, I found myself searching for Mr. Darcy as I had at Lady Bearing's ball.

Then, all at once, I saw him.

His dark hair and strong jaw were unmistakable, as was the look in his eyes as he met my gaze. The gentleman beside him I recognized as Mr. Bingley—the gentleman who had taken Mr. Darcy away from me in London.

Delightful.

As he spotted me, Mr. Bingley's expression changed, and then I realized that he was looking at Jane.

I glanced at my sister as the gentleman strode toward us and then nudged her with my elbow.

"Jane—" I whispered.

But I was not fast enough. Charles Bingley and Mr. Darcy bowed almost in unison as they came upon us.

"Miss Elizabeth, Miss Jane," Mr. Darcy said. "You both look lovely this evening. Please permit me to introduce my friend, Mr. Charles Bingley."

"Mr. Bingley, Papa tells us that you have taken on the lease at Netherfield Park," Jane said with a smile.

"I have, indeed," he blurted out. "It is a fine estate."

"Indeed, if a little dusty," I said.

Charles Bingley laughed and I caught my sister's smile out of the corner of my eye. "A little cleaning will put it right," he said. "I do not mind a little dust when there is grandeur beneath."

"Indeed," Jane said. "I cannot recall when it was last occupied. The caretaker will be glad of your presence there."

"Miss Bennet," Mr. Bingley said hastily. "Will you dance?"

"We have only just arrived," I said in surprise. But Jane winked at me and laid her hand upon Mr. Bingley's proffered arm.

"I would be delighted," she said.

My mouth dropped open as I watched my sister walk away toward the dance floor with Mr. Bingley.

"He seems very taken with her," Mr. Darcy murmured.

"She is very pretty," I replied. "He would not be the first to fall head over heels in love with her after two dances."

"Is that so?"

I glanced at the gentleman at my side, suddenly suspicious of his question. "No, I do not mean it in a scandalous manner. It is only— Jane is a good person with a lovely, trusting, manner. It is not difficult to see why men fall in love with her so quickly."

"But she has not accepted any proposals?"

"No, indeed," I replied. "She did consider one last summer, but it came to nothing after the young man was sent to Brighton to the regiment there."

"A pity."

"Not entirely," I replied with a smile. "He was a very dull sort of gentleman, and he was not very forthcoming on his family history. I believe she was relieved when he went to Brighton."

"I see."

"Your friend," I said. "Is he anything like you?"

He regarded me with a raised eyebrow. "Like me?"

"Is he an arrogant and entitled gentleman who believes that everyone exists to cater to his every whim?" I wanted to smile, but I forced myself to stay serious. I did enjoy teasing him. And it was the truth, after all.

The gentleman favored me with a wry smile. "Indeed not," he said. "Charles is as different to me as... As a rose is to a dandelion."

"And who of the two of you is the dandelion, Mr. Darcy?"

"I— That is not a successful comparison..."

"Indeed not," I said. "I find roses lacking in all usefulness aside from their perfume, and even that does not last. Full of pretense with no substance. Dandelions, however—why, bees love them. They make a passable wine, and add brightness to the most desolate of roadsides. The rabbits love them, and when they are gone to seed, they delight children as they blow on the puffs..."

"You are mocking me now," he said.

I smiled but said nothing more. He was only half correct.

We stood together, watching the dancers as they moved to the music. Jane and Mr. Bingley made a handsome couple, and I was not surprised to see a smile on Jane's beautiful face.

"Would you dance, Miss Bennet?" Mr. Darcy asked.

"I suppose we must," I sighed.

"We do not have to if you do not wish it."

I glanced over his shoulder. "I do not wish to speak to anyone else about our engagement," I said. "And Lady Lucas is bearing down upon us like a ship... So, we must dance to avoid her."

"Indeed," he said quickly as he offered me his elbow. I laid my hand upon it and we walked to the dance floor together at a quick pace, leaving Lady Lucas behind.

We took our positions and I set my hand in his as the dance began. As we danced, I found myself drawn to Mr. Darcy in a way that surprised me and I felt some of my initial prickliness begin to fade away. We talked in brief snatches as we moved through the steps of the dance and I surprised myself by laughing at some of his observations.

For the first time since this whole ordeal began, I found myself enjoying his company.

As the dance came to an end, I found myself feeling regretful. I did not want the conversation to end. I hoped that he felt the same way, but I could not tell.

We parted ways when the music stopped and I turned to him with a smile upon my face—a genuine one this time.

"Thank you for the dance, Mr. Darcy," I said. "It was pleasant."

"Pleasant? Surely it was more than that," he said, offering me a small smile.

"It was," I admitted. "Very much so."

For a moment, there was an awkward silence between us, but thankfully it was broken by the sound of laughter from across the room.

We both turned to see Jane and Mr. Bingley coming towards us, their faces lit up with joy.

"Miss Elizabeth!" Mr. Bingley exclaimed as he reached us. "I have been looking for you everywhere. You simply must come and meet my sisters Caroline and Louisa. They have talked of nothing else but meeting you."

I felt my smile falter just a little. I did not want to meet anyone new tonight... especially any of Mr. Darcy's acquaintances. I was not ready. "Is that so," I said. "Well, I cannot ignore such attention."

As Mr. Bingley led me away, I noticed two unfamiliar faces in the crowd. Two women dressed far too elegantly for a Hertfordshire ball, with fake smiles plastered on their faces and dyed ostrich feathers bobbing above their elaborate hairstyles.

"Ah, there you are," Mr. Bingley said. "Caroline, Louisa—This is Miss Elizabeth Bennet. You have already heard a great deal about her from Mr. Darcy, and I am very pleased to finally be able to make this introduction."

"Miss Elizabeth Bennet," Louisa Hurst said with a smooth smile. "How charming you look."

"I shall leave you ladies to get acquainted," Mr. Bingley said. "I shall fetch some refreshment."

Caroline Bingley's smile was cold, and her beauty had an edge to it that made me feel like a rabbit being chased by hawks.

"What a wonderful gathering," she said. "We do not have anything like this in London, do we, Louisa?"

"Certainly not," her sister replied.

"I do hope that you will enjoy your stay in Hertfordshire," I managed. "Netherfield Park is beautiful."

"It is shabby and old and drafty," Caroline said. "It is nothing to our London home, but Charles is smitten with it."

"He seems smitten with other things, too," Louisa observed smoothly.

I glanced over my shoulder and saw Mr. Bingley speaking to my sister. They looked very taken with each other, and I could not help but feel my heart lift with happiness for Jane.

"But of course, Charles alway did have a more common taste, did he not?" Caroline's smile was sharp. "Mr. Darcy, however, I always expected that he would have finer taste. Do you not agree, Miss Bennet?"

I was taken aback by her bluntness. "Excuse me?"

"Oh, please do not pretend ignorance," Caroline said with a smirk. "We all know that Mr. Darcy has taken a liking to you, despite your inferior connections and lack of fortune."

My cheeks burned with indignation. "Mr. Darcy's opinion of me is none of your concern," I said tersely.

"On the contrary," Louisa said smoothly. "As Mr. Darcy's close acquaintances, it is very much our concern who he chooses to associate himself with. Especially when it comes to an engagement."

"And is it not his own choice to make?" I asked, feeling more and more uncomfortable with this conversation.

"Of course it is," Caroline said with a dismissive wave of her hand. "But we cannot help but be concerned for his well-being and reputation."

"I believe Mr. Darcy is perfectly capable of making his own decisions," I said firmly. "Now if you will excuse me, I must go find my sister."

I turned to leave but Caroline's voice stopped me in my tracks.

"Just remember, Miss Elizabeth," she said with a sly smile. "Mr. Darcy may have taken a liking to you now, but he has a history of changing his mind about women."

I stiffened as I heard Caroline's words, feeling a hot wave of anger wash over me. I did not need to know whom they were speaking of, and I did not wish to know.

"If you will excuse me, it was lovely to meet you both, but I must find my sister. Good evening, ladies," I said through gritted teeth before turning on my heel and walking briskly away.

I could hear their laughter trailing after me, but I pushed it out of my mind as I searched the crowd for Jane. When I finally spotted her, she was still talking to Mr. Bingley, her eyes shining with happiness.

I could not interrupt their conversation with my petty grievances. Caroline and Louisa had set out to hurt my feelings, and I would not give them the satisfaction of seeing that their barbs had hit their mark.

I walked through the ballroom and out the double doors that led to the courtyard. Torches had been set at intervals in the sparse gardens that had been planted only the season before.

Furious, I marched through the gravel and kicked at a clump of weeds that had sprung up through the pale stones.

"Elizabeth—"

Mr. Darcy had followed me.

"Are these women your *friends*?" I snapped without turning around.

"They are Charles' sisters," he said.

"That does not answer my question," I retorted.

"No, I suppose it does not."

"They are horrid vultures," I said and pointed accusingly at the hall. "I do not want *my* sister anywhere near them!"

"What did they say to you?"

"Nothing that concerns you," I snapped. "But then again, perhaps it does. Caroline Bingley, no mystery as to why she is unmarried, was kind enough to tell me that she was surprised that a woman like me would catch your attention, as I am neither well connected, nor in possession of a fortune, nor do I have a name that can be spoken in the ballrooms of London with any hope of recognition. But she did assure me that your interest would wane soon enough. Such a comfort."

"Caroline is—"

"A snake," I snapped. "Tell me, Mr. Darcy, truthfully—what was it about me that made you decide to use me for your deception? Was there something I said, or perhaps it was the color of my gown— I borrowed that gown from Lady Bearing's daughter, you know—"

"You were entirely unlike anyone else I had ever met," he said without hesitation.

I blinked at him in surprise.

"I beg your pardon?"

"That is it," he said. "I did not care who your family was, or what fortune you might have... only that you were unlike anyone I had ever met."

I stared at him as disbelief and curiosity coursed through me. "And how *exactly* am I unlike anyone else you have ever met?" I asked. "We barely spoke that night."

Mr. Darcy took a deep breath and looked up at the moon that hung in the dark sky above us. "I must admit that you made an impression upon me that night... But my opinions have remained unchanged as I have spoken to you more and feel that we have come to know each other better..."

"Have we," I said carefully.

"You are not afraid to speak your mind, no matter the situation. You are intelligent, quick-witted and have a sense of humor that catches me off-guard. You are fiercely independent, unafraid to stand up for yourself or others. You are everything that I have been searching for in a partner, Elizabeth. Everything I did not know I was searching for..."

I stared at him for a long moment before I could bear it no longer and had to look away. "I see," was all I could say, but I could hear the waver in my own voice and cursed myself for it.

"I know that this may seem sudden, and I understand if you need some time to consider my words," he said evenly. "But I cannot hide my feelings any longer. Our acquaintance began as an accident— Because of my..."

"Arrogance," I finished.

He smiled and shook my head. "My arrogance, as you say."

"I appreciate your honesty," I said finally, turning back to face him. "But there are obstacles between us that cannot be simply brushed aside."

"What obstacles?" he asked.

"Your pride, for one," I said.

He winced at that, and I felt somewhat better to have wounded him, even a little.

"And what makes you think that my pride is an obstacle?"

"You must know how you come across to others," I said bluntly. "You are aloof and condescending."

"Am I?" He seemed surprised by it. "I cannot deny that I have acted in such a manner in the past," he finally admitted.

I stared at him incredulously. "In the *past*... does this mean that you are willing to change? That is a surprising admission from you, Mr. Darcy."

He paused, as though he was considering his next words carefully. "Elizabeth, I have come to realize that societal norms and expectations are not what truly matters in life. What matters is love and happiness, and I believe that we could find that together."

I could not stop the derisive noise that left my lips. "And what about your family's expectations of you? They surely would not approve of a match with someone like me. When Lady Catherine de Bourgh learns of my connections and my true station in life, she will withdraw all of her begrudging politeness. If it can even be called such."

"My family's approval is not something that I seek nor need," Mr. Darcy said firmly. "I have always been my own person, and I refuse to let their prejudices dictate my happiness."

Was this really the same gentleman who had stolen my likeness for his own lies? I did not know this gentleman. "You truly mean this," I said softly.

"I do," he replied as he reached out to take my hand in his. "Elizabeth, will you give me the chance to prove myself worthy of your esteem?"

"I do not have a choice in this matter," I said bitterly. "So I suppose that I must." My words were angry, but I did not pull my hand away. I could not.

"Shall we return to the ball?" he asked.

I made a face. "Must we?"

"There is nothing in the world that will infuriate Caroline more than to see you happy," he said. "And if you are dancing with me, she will be even more frustrated that her attempts to wound you have failed."

"Is that so," I murmured. Angering Caroline would be a heady tonic, indeed. "Then we simply must return to the ball. We have missed far too many dances already."

I tightened my grip on his hand and then released it.

"Thank you, Mr. Darcy—"

"William, please," he said.

"William," I repeated, his name felt strange on my tongue. Strange but somehow wonderful at the same time. "When I thought of my future, this was not... this was not what I wished for myself."

"What did you wish?"

I bit my lip as I tried to decide what to say. "I wished for the very deepest love. I always said that I would never marry except on that one condition... And now, here I am, engaged to a gentleman who pretended that we—" I laughed shortly. "But I know now that such a thing is impossible."

"What if it were *not* impossible?"

I stared at him. "What?"

"What if it were not impossible?"

I laughed again. "What are you saying?"

"Love is not a simple thing," he said. "The greatest love is not something that one falls into by accident. It is... earned. It is cultivated... It is coaxed to grow where once you might have thought that nothing would ever take root."

"More gardening metaphors, William? You are not very adept at them."

"I am not," he admitted. "But perhaps you might teach me."

I snorted. "Come, there is a chill in the air, and I have the urge to dance until dawn comes over the horizon. Will you indulge me?"

I felt reckless and brave. What did I have to lose now? Nothing.

"I shall," he replied. "Will you come inside, Miss Bennet?"

"Happily, Mr. Darcy."

eleven

RETURNING HOME to Longbourn after the regimental ball was usually a tepid affair. Lydia and Kitty would prattle on about the officers they had danced with and how handsome all of the gentlemen were in their regimental coats... but that evening, the only thing that anyone wished to talk about was Mr. Bingley.

Jane and Mr. Darcy's friend had danced for most of the evening, and it did not take long for the gossips to begin their assumptions as to how long it would be before an engagement followed.

Such things were usually easy to predict.

An officer and a young lady would engage in some polite flirtation in town.

Then at the next available social event they would dance— if it was not to be, only one dance would be had. But if there was a spark of attraction, perhaps there would be three or four dances... never in a row, of course, but just the same. People would be watching and taking note.

In the weeks that followed the dances, the gentleman

would enquire after her family and perhaps pay a visit or two to the family home.

It was then a foregone conclusion that one of those visits would include a discussion of dowry and courtship with the gentleman of the house—and then, an engagement and a marriage to follow quickly.

Simple.

Every engagement in Hertfordshire had progressed as such.

It was what I had always expected for myself... and for my sisters.

I had always imagined that I would be able to tell my own children the story of the great love I had found with their father —but that was a fantasy, too. How could I tell anyone the truth about how Mr. Darcy and I had met. Jane and Mr. Bingley were the only ones who knew the entire truth... and it would have to stay that way.

Mama was, of course, more than thrilled by Mr. Bingley's attentions toward Jane, and she sat as proudly as a queen in her chair in the parlor the following morning while the younger girls gossiped and imagined what might happen in the coming weeks.

"Who would have thought," Mama mused. "My two eldest girls, married to wealthy gentlemen before the year is out. And to think that I was so concerned about having one of you marry Mr. Collins— I had even considered offering Kitty to him."

"Mama," Kitty cried. "You would not have done so!"

"Oh, but I would have," our mother exclaimed, "had he not hustled over to Lucas Lodge within hours of Lizzy's refusal of him! I daresay Lady Lucas would have married them in her own garden if she could have done so that very day! The nerve."

It was astounding how quickly my mother could pivot from victim to victor in the space of a few hours of conversation.

But now that everyone she knew was buzzing with the

news of my own engagement—much to my chagrin—my mother was in her glory. Lady Lucas with all of her connections could only boast that her daughter was the wife of a clergyman, after all...

The days after the regimental ball passed in a blur. Jane was invited to Netherfield Park to take tea with Mr. Bingley's loathsome sisters, an invitation which I chose to decline when Jane asked me to accompany her. I did feel somewhat guilty for it, but I could not bear to look Caroline Bingley in the face again.

But when Jane returned from Netherfield Park that day, she looked rather pale. I worried at once that something had happened and I rushed out to meet her.

"Jane— Whatever is the matter? Did Caroline Bingley say something horrid to you? That woman..."

"No, no," Jane said quickly. "Nothing like that. Mr. Bingley's sisters were wonderfully accommodating and pleasant."

I did not believe it for a moment, but Jane was far too sweet to complain about anything.

"Then what is it?"

Jane glanced at the house and then took hold of my hand.

"I believe... I believe that I saw Mr. Collins come to Netherfield Park," she whispered.

"What?"

My voice echoed in the still air and Jane hushed me.

"Keep your voice down. I may be mistaken... of course I do hope that I am."

I shook my head. "You never forget a face, Jane. If you think it was him, then it most certainly must be. But what business would he have with Mr. Bingley?"

"I do not know," Jane said. "But I believe it will not be long before we have a visit from our dear cousin."

She grimaced at those last words and I felt icy dread settle over my shoulders.

"We must tell Mama," I said, though I dreaded that conversation as well.

Jane nodded and laced her arm through mine. She leaned against me as we walked back toward the house and she told me of the light gossip that had been discussed over tea with Mr. Bingley's sisters.

"Caroline made several mentions of Mr. Darcy, and his sister Georgiana," Jane said.

"Oh? In what— In what manner?"

"Highly complementary, of course, though she did mention that she had wished for her brother to court Miss Darcy— though from their description of her she does sound very young. Perhaps Kitty's age."

"Indeed," I said. "That is quite assumptive of her, is it not? Mr. Bingley has, very specifically, shown you particular favor."

"Now, Lizzy," Jane said. "I do not think she meant anything by it..."

"I do," I muttered. "I do not trust her. She went out of her way to remind me that our family's social standing and connections are not good enough—"

"I remember," Jane said with a sigh. "Thankfully, her opinion does not matter to Mr. Darcy. And in any case, there is nothing that can be done about it now."

"No, indeed," I murmured. But something in the back of my mind was ringing an alarm bell. Mr. Collins' arrival at Netherfield Park could only mean that a visit to Longbourn was imminent—*but why?*

THE FOLLOWING DAY, I received the answer I was looking for. But it was far from the answer I wished it to be.

A note arrived in the morning over breakfast, addressed to Papa.

He came into the parlor with a stern look upon his face and I was instantly worried. "Papa, what is it?" I asked.

"You shall hear," he said. "My esteemed cousin, etcetera etcetera, I find myself with no option but to visit Longbourn to conduct a thorough accounting of the household. My patroness, Lady Catherine de Bourgh, has expressed an interest in my acquisition and should like to see it for herself to determine its fitness and appropriateness for a gentleman of my standing."

"Appropriateness," Mama cried. "Whatever does that mean!"

"My dear wife," Papa said calmly, "he means to assess whether or not he will keep the property or sell it when I am gone."

"Oh, Mr. Bennet," our mother wailed. "You cannot allow this!"

"It seems that I must," Papa said. "Come along girls, we must make the house presentable for Mr. Collins and Lady Catherine de Bourgh's visit."

"But when are they coming?" I asked.

My father held out the letter and I took it from his hands as he left the parlor to return to his study. The sound of the door slamming shut was muffled by the noise in the room as my sisters wailed and moaned about their impending doom.

"He is coming today," I said to Jane as I read over the parson's words. "This afternoon."

"Then we must hurry," Jane said firmly. She clapped her hands to command the attention of the room. "Come now, girls. This is no time to be hysterical. We must straighten up this room. Go and make your beds and wash your faces. If Mr. Collins and Lady Catherine are coming here, we must be presentable."

I took a deep breath and pressed my hands against my skirts to calm myself.

"It will all be over soon," Jane murmured. I nodded and set to work helping her tidy the parlor while our mother wailed and flapped her hands in the background.

"Whatever shall we do," she cried.

"Whatever we must, Mama," Jane said. "Now, please, find some cheer for the girls."

Mama dabbed her eyes with her handkerchief and tried to compose herself.

If we were to be descended upon, we would be prepared.

WE DID NOT HAVE long to wait.

Lydia and Kitty had only just come back down to the parlor after changing their gowns and washing their faces when a carriage pulled into the courtyard.

Through the window we watched Mr. Collins alight from the carriage and offer his hand to the other occupant. Lady Catherine de Bourgh, surveyed the house with a critical eye before she accepted his assistance to step down to the gravel.

As her Ladyship moved toward the house, two horses cantered into the courtyard, gravel kicking up from their hooves as the rider's brought them to a stop.

"It is Mr. Darcy," Kitty whispered loudly.

"And Mr. Bingley!" Lydia echoed.

Mrs. Hill rushed to the front door to open it as Mr. Collins approached the house with Lady Catherine following behind at a slower, more menacing, pace.

"Ah, Mrs. Bennet," Mr. Collins said with a bow as he entered the drawing room. "Please allow me to introduce Lady Catherine de Bourgh, my esteemed patroness."

My mother looked as though she was about to faint from

nervousness as she curtsied deeply in an effort to compose herself before speaking.

"Thank you, Lady Catherine," she said in a voice that shook only a little. "We are honored by your visit."

Lady Catherine looked around the room with a scowl on her face as if she were taking stock of everything in it, including its inhabitants.

"I must say, Mrs. Bennet, that I expected more from an estate such as this one," Lady Catherine said with a sniff. "The furniture is outdated and the decor lacking in taste."

I stiffened at the older woman's brisk assessment of the house and though I tried to keep my emotions in check, my cheeks burned with anger. Mr. Darcy took his place beside me, and I could not deny that I felt comforted by his presence even though I was confused by his attendance at this humiliating meeting.

"Your daughter, Elizabeth, has formed an attachment with my nephew," Lady Catherine said coldly.

"Indeed," my mother replied brightly, happy for the change in the direction of the conversation. "They are engaged to be married. Here in Hertfordshire."

"Is that so," Lady Catherine replied in an icy tone.

"Indeed, it is," my mother continued. "The parson has presided over every event in this area since the girls were very young. It would only be proper that he should perform their marriages, too."

Lady Catherine's ringed fingers tapped against the silver top of her cane with a sharp sound that only served to punctuate the silence.

"Mr. Collins," she said. "I do not believe that this house is worth the investment it would require to bring it to a proper standard." She spoke as though there was no one else in the room, and my spine straightened as she moved through the drawing room.

"Even the pianoforte would not fetch much of a price," she mused as she rubbed her finger along the wooden edge of the instrument and frowned at the dust she imagined she saw there.

"Indeed, your Ladyship," Mr. Collins simpered.

My fists clenched at my sides as I struggled to maintain control. Lady Catherine wanted me to lose my temper and prove that I was not worthy of Mr. Darcy's affections. I would not give her the satisfaction of it.

"Your Ladyship," Mr. Darcy said in a tone that brooked no argument. "I believe it is time for you to leave. Your visit has caused enough disturbance in this household and it is clear that you have no respect for those who live here."

Lady Catherine's eyes widened in shock, clearly unaccustomed to being spoken to in such a manner and even I could not resist the urge to turn my head to look at him. This was... unexpected to say the least.

"I beg your pardon?" she spluttered.

"You heard me correctly," the gentleman continued, his voice growing stronger with each passing second. "Your constant insults towards the home of my future wife and the family she loves are unacceptable. I will not tolerate any more of your behavior."

My mother let out a choked gasp, obviously shocked at his words, but I felt nothing but pride in what he was saying.

Lady Catherine drew herself up to her full height and glared at her nephew with an intensity that would have made lesser men falter.

"Do you realize who I am?" she spat.

"I am well aware of who you are," Mr. Darcy said calmly.

"And I am also aware that your title does not give you the right to insult those around you."

"Nephew," she said, her eyes narrowing. "This engagement of yours... I will not tolerate it. You will throw off this pretense at once and deny this young woman her grasping search for a wealthy gentleman. I know this type of woman very well, indeed. One of them very nearly saw her way to marrying Lord de Bourgh before he met me."

"A pity, indeed," Mr. Darcy said coldly.

"I beg your pardon—"

"You heard me quite well, I think," he said. "I *shall* not, and I *will* not cast this woman aside. She is the one I have chosen to be my wife and to be the Mistress of Pemberley. You have no say in this matter." Mr. Darcy turned to the parson. "Mr. Collins, you are not welcome here. Longbourn may be yours by entailment, but your presence is no longer required. If you wish to visit this estate, you must write to *me* to ask for permission, and your visits will be supervised."

The parson's mouth opened and closed soundlessly.

"I suggest very strongly that you carefully consider your next steps," I said warningly.

"We shall go at once to Lucas Lodge," Lady Catherine snapped. "Lady Lucas will be very honored to welcome us."

"I'm certain that she will be," Mr. Darcy said.

Lady Catherine de Bourgh stood there for a moment longer, her cold eyes still narrowed and her breathing heavy. The entire room held its breath as she turned on her heel and stormed out of the room with Mr. Collins scurrying after her like a loyal lapdog.

The room was silent for a moment until my mother let out a long sigh and sank into a chair. I could hold myself back no longer and threw myself against Mr. Darcy. I could scarcely breathe through my relief.

"I cannot believe you did that," I whispered to him.

"I could not let her continue to insult your family and your home," he replied softly. He kissed my forehead briefly and I closed my eyes as a strange feeling coursed through me.

"But to speak to Lady Catherine de Bourgh in such a manner..." My mother's words trailed off, clearly stunned by the gentleman's actions.

"I cannot stand by and allow anyone to treat those that I care for in such a manner," the gentleman said firmly.

"What will happen now?" Jane asked. She sat on the couch beside Mr. Bingley, and I smiled to see them sitting so close together, their hands almost touching on the cushions between them.

"Lady Catherine will make a good deal of noise about my rudeness," Mr. Darcy said. "She will go to Lucas Lodge and she will tell anyone who will listen about my insolence and the rudeness of the Bennet family—but your neighbors know you well. They will not take such things to heart."

"I do hope not," my mother exclaimed.

"And as for Mr. Collins," Mr. Darcy continued, "he will think twice before he insults anyone in this household again. And if he does, he will find himself completely unwelcome here."

"I cannot thank you enough, Mr. Darcy," I said in a voice that was breathless with surprise at his outburst. "You stood up for us all."

"I will always stand up for what is right," he replied, "and I will always defend those I care for."

"Well, that was certainly an exciting visit," Mr. Bingley said with a chuckle. "I do believe we must return to Netherfield Park. Caroline will not take kindly to this change of plans..."

"Indeed," Mr. Darcy said. He grasped my hand gently. "We shall speak soon."

All I could do was nod. How could I say anything more—my

emotions were a confused jumble of pride, gratitude, and... perhaps even love.

The gentlemen bid us good day and my mother kissed their cheeks and exclaimed over their bravery in coming to our aid. Mr. Bingley grinned as though it had been he who had faced down Lady Catherine de Bourgh, and I was, once again, struck by the quiet strength of the gentleman who would be my husband.

As they departed I felt a sudden pang.

"Lizzy— you should go and talk to him," Jane said as we watched the gentlemen untie their horses from the fence.

"I should— what?"

Jane pushed me toward the door. "Go!"

I stumbled slightly as I rushed out of the house, my heart pounding in my chest as I rushed after the gentlemen.

"Mr. Darcy— William!" I called out.

Mr. Bingley continued to lead his horse down the road as Mr. Darcy turned back to look at me.

"Elizabeth—"

"I— I wanted to speak to you," I said breathlessly as I reached him. "I wanted to— I wanted to apologize."

My cheeks were warm, and I could barely breathe from the exertion and the effect of being so close to him—*how could I allow my emotions to govern me so completely?*

"Apologize, for what?"

"I did not... I did not give you the chance you deserved," I said. "To make things right. I was cruel to you—"

The gentleman shook my head and took my hands in his. "There is no apology to be made. The fault in this was all mine. If it were not for me, your life would be unchanged, and now you are tied to—"

"The very gentleman that I did not know I needed," I finished.

"Elizabeth—"

"William?"

The gentleman's dark eyes, flecked with gray that I had not noticed before, held mine with a gentle intensity that I could not look away from.

"Will you marry me?" he asked.

My heart might have stopped beating at that moment.

"What?" I whispered.

"You were right," he said. "When you were shouting at me so many weeks ago... You were quite correct. I have never asked you to marry me. Well, now I have done it." he paused for just a moment. Long enough for my heart to catch up with my head.

"Ask me again," I whispered.

"Elizabeth Bennet," he said with a smile. "You are everything I never knew that I needed in my life... Will you marry me? Will you be my wife?"

I looked down at our clasped hands and then back up at him. I had a fleeting thought that I should reject him... that I could make everything right again and return to my life. A life— without him. But I could never do it.

I nodded. "I will."

"You will?"

"Yes."

It was only a whisper, but it was enough.

He bent his head to kiss me, but I was already rising up on my toes to meet his lips. The kiss was all too brief, but the sweetness of it lingered on my lips as I pulled away.

"I shall see you tomorrow," I whispered. "Perhaps we might speak more about our wedding plans."

The gentleman nodded, clearly lost for words.

My heart pounded in my chest as I pulled my hands from his grasp and grinned at him. I barely recognized myself. Barely knew how to comprehend what had just happened and how I felt... this was true. This was the very deepest love that I had been searching for... I knew it now.

As I turned and ran back to the house I heard a joyful whoop from behind me. I glanced over my shoulder to see Mr. Bingley clap his friend on the shoulder hard enough to make him stumble and I laughed as I ran harder for the house.

It had been an impossible thing, this lie he had asked me to partake in.

But I knew better now. It was a simple thing, love. And while I did not understand it any better now than I did when I had first set eyes upon him at Lady Bearing's ball, I had some idea of how it felt.

That was enough for me.

THE END

Milton Keynes UK
Ingram Content Group UK Ltd.
UKHW020730120923
428521UK00014B/503